THE ORIGIN OF SWORD MASTER

SECOND CHANCES

A catalogue record for this work is available from the National Library of Australia

Second Chances
Book 1
The Origin of Sword Master
ISBN: 978-0-6457244-7-9 (paperback)

Cover illustration Alisa Beagley
Typesetting Luke Harris

Printed by IngramSpark Australia

THE ORIGIN OF SWORD MASTER

SECOND CHANCES

ALISA BEAGLEY

Character Profiles

Rifle Power

Sword Master

James Power

Tiger-eye

Grandfather Power

Tyler Power

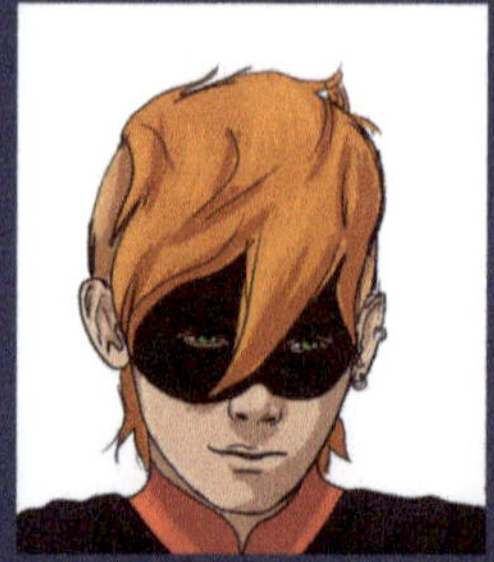

Flame

Tilly Summers

Dr Tener

Amelia Young

Jason Young

Kaine Young

Rob Peterson

Fiona Dan

Ninja Star

Killer Kaine

Andrew Peters

Tekno

CONTENTS

Fire

Rifle and Tyler tumbled across the carpeted floor with their dad, Jason, laughing hard as they attempted to pin him down. With identical cheeky grins, vibrant red hair and bright green eyes, it was easy to tell they were twins.

'You little rascals!' exclaimed Jason with a grin, flipping both boys onto the floor beside him. 'Okay. It's time for bed, Ninja Warriors.'

'Yes, Dad,' chorused the twins disappointedly, allowing Jason to lead them to their room.

'C'mon Mum!' they called. 'Say goodnight to us now.'

'Coming,' replied Amelia, calling out from their big brother's room.

Kaine was bent over his Calculus worksheets, scribbling down answers as though completing preschool maths.

'Goodnight, my little genius,' murmured Amelia, kissing him on the forehead. Kaine smiled up at her.

'Goodnight, Mum,' he responded, putting away his work and climbing into bed. Amelia walked out of the room, switching off the light on the way. She didn't notice Kaine holding a box of matches and pieces of paper under the sheets.

Amelia tucked the twins into bed and headed to the couch, where Jason sat watching the TV.

Later that night, Jason awoke to the sound of crackling flames. He jumped out of bed and coughed as the overwhelming smell of smoke filled his nostrils.

'The boys... Fire near their rooms!' he choked, frantically waking Amelia. They ran toward the sound of crackling and splitting wood.

Kaine stumbled out of his room.

'Come on, Mum, get out,' he tugged Amelia's arm in the opposite direction of the fire.

'No, I need to get the twins,' protested Amelia, heading back for the fire.

'Mum, no,' whispered Kaine, horror crossing his face. 'Mum! Stop it!' He pulled her backward, digging his heels into the floor.

'Quit it, Kaine! The boys are in danger,' scolded Amelia. She pulled herself free of her persistent son's grasp and slipped through a gap in the debris and flames that had almost blocked the door of the twins' room. Before Jason could follow, more debris crumbled behind her.

'Mum!' screamed Kaine, sounding almost as angry as distraught. 'How could you? You'll kill yourself!' Snatching a small picture frame off the wall, he fled out of the house.

'Amelia!' Jason felt his heart skip a beat. He began panicking when there was no immediate response. 'Amelia, are you all right?'

'I'm okay... Get outside!' she yelled. 'I'll get the twins down to you by the window.'

Jason sprinted out to the window, where Amelia lowered first Tyler, then Rifle, down to his outstretched arms.

'Go on, get away from here as fast as you can,' urged Jason, his eyes flicking around as if searching for something... or someone.

'But Dad...' began Rifle, setting up a whinge that Tyler took up too.

'No 'buts'. Go!' Jason's voice took on a sharp tone. 'It's too dangerous here. Get as far away as possible.' He reached for Amelia but looked back to find the twins still there.

'Leave now!' yelled Jason, and they hesitantly began to walk away. A blast of heat shot out of the building as a

wall crumbled. The twins fled from the house, coughing and crying.

Escaping the heat was the only thing on their minds at that moment. When they reached a place far enough from the fire, Rifle glanced back. He cried out in alarm as the house collapsed, reduced to a burning wreck. The cloud of dust and debris that exploded into the air hid everything, and it was impossible to tell if his parents had made it out of there.

'Mum! Dad!' he cried, tears streaming down his face. He wanted to return to the house to find his parents, but Tyler's strong hand held him back.

'There's nothing we can do. Come on, Rifle,' insisted Tyler, tugging at his arm. A shadowed figure with blond hair caught Rifle's attention.

'Is that Kaine?' squinted Rifle, trying to clear his eyes of the dust and smoke. 'Kaine!' The figure didn't respond but ducked away. Rifle quickly pursued, and Tyler followed, not wanting to be left alone.

Each time they thought they'd lost the figure, he'd appear somewhere and wait for them to notice him before running on. It seemed like he wanted them to follow, and Rifle continued to call Kaine's name at intervals. He didn't understand why his older brother wouldn't answer. It just didn't make any sense at all.

*   *   *

Jason stumbled to a stop, a safe distance from the house. He'd heard the boys calling him, but he couldn't respond or approach them while searching for Amelia in the blistering heat and thick smoke. He could hardly even find his way out of the rubble, and by the time he did, the twins had disappeared. Had they even made it out of there? The odds that they had escaped in time were slim, especially with their reluctance to leave. His mind felt numb about the latest events, and his legs had turned to jelly. He struggled to breathe without coughing.

People gathered on the street in front of the burning house, and the first neighbour to have arrived called the fire brigade. Before long, the wail of an emergency vehicle filled the air, to the relief of everyone there. The iconic red truck pulled up, and firefighters rushed out to extinguish the blaze. Soon after, an ambulance came for him, with paramedics loading him on board for smoke inhalation and burns.

'My wife... she was in there when it collapsed,' gasped Jason, 'and my boys... I don't know where... they've gone.'

Paramedics urged him to remain quiet as they transported him to the hospital. He tried to focus, but his mind was racing until the fluids from the IV in his arm forced his consciousness to drift away.

Chapter 2

The Letter

A mysterious figure prowled through the streets, sticking to the shadows and remaining on high alert. An enigma to the citizens of Umbre City and a nightmare for criminals, he was a force to be reckoned with. His mask hid his civilian identity as he fought crime every night.

A man, all in black and cradling a hidden object, caught his attention, and the vigilante silently approached him. People usually avoided being out on the streets past sundown due to the criminals that emerged after that time. The man stood outside an antiques store, peering in the window. As the man raised a fist to smash the window, the vigilante leaped out of the shadows and knocked him to the ground.

'What were you doing?' growled the vigilante. 'It's 11pm. You should be home, not trying to vandalise public property.'

'I-I had to get your attention somehow. You're not exactly easy to locate, you know,' stammered the man,

shakily rising to his feet. 'Some crazy kid forced me to find you to give you this. He said he'd kill me if I didn't do as he asked.' He held out a somewhat crumpled page that had been ripped out of a textbook.

Grabbing the front of the man's shirt to ensure he wouldn't make a run for it, the vigilante snatched the page, scanning his eyes over the neat writing. Its contents piqued his interest.

'Do you know who wrote this?' asked the vigilante.

'No, but he was just a kid. Wearing pyjamas,' offered the man.

'That's just about every kid in the city at this time of night,' the vigilante grumbled, rolling his eyes. 'If you don't have any *useful* information for me, you can leave now. Go home.' He gave the man a shove and walked away, leaving him standing there stunned. He knew he was being unreasonably impolite with the man, but he wanted the man to know that he wasn't happy about the method of gaining his attention. There was no excuse for crime.

Straightening out the page, he began reading it in earnest.

'To Tiger-eye, please save my brothers. They are twins who have escaped a house fire, and our home and parents are gone now. My brothers have no relations to care for them and no friends who would do that either. You will find my brothers under the bridge on the outskirts of the city. You will know them because

Rifle wears blue and Tyler wears red. I know you have enough money to provide for them and a house that will give them a safe place to stay. I need you to look after them, or they will die living in the streets alone. I'm fine on my own, but they aren't.'

There was no signature or name to show who wrote the letter.

The vigilante folded the page into a neat square that fit in a pouch on his belt and strode purposefully through the streets toward the bridge.

The note could very well be someone just messing with his time, but he had to make sure. If there really were two boys on the streets, he wouldn't forgive himself should they come to any harm.

Lightning Strike

The twins had been running all day, following their silent and shadowed leader. Their stomachs growled in hunger, and they could hardly move a step further from exhaustion.

At that point, the kid that Rifle thought was Kaine disappeared and didn't show himself again, leaving them under a bridge in a completely unfamiliar part of the city. They settled under the large concrete structure, staring out into the pouring rain and shivering as thunder growled overhead. The longer they rested under the bridge watching the dismal weather, the more Rifle's spirits sunk.

'We're so far from home,' said Rifle softly.

'Just think, at least we have each other,' began Tyler. He couldn't bear the miserable silence anymore.

'Where's Kaine?' sniffed Rifle. 'I'd even settle for his boring company right now. Why didn't he talk to us and why did he lead us here?'

'You don't even know if it was actually him,' reasoned Tyler.

'It looked like him,' frowned Rifle stubbornly, but he didn't have the energy to argue with Tyler.

The twins watched the rain for a while longer before they decided to continue searching for food.

As they wandered out into the storm, lightning crackled down and struck Rifle with a deafening boom. Electricity coursed through his body, deflecting off him and hitting Tyler as well. When the lightning receded, the twins were dazed, but surprisingly unharmed.

'What just happened?' mumbled Rifle slowly, patting down his frizzed-up hair.

'You zapped me!' accused Tyler angrily, tears forming in his big green eyes. 'It hurt.'

'I didn't mean to... I couldn't help it.' They scampered back into the shelter of the bridge. Rifle plonked down, trying to stop his hands from shaking.

'You look pale,' commented Tyler. 'Are you cold?'

When Tyler lifted his hands, they sparked, and small flames appeared on his fingertips.

'Fire!' yelped Rifle, shuffling away on his backside.

'Cool,' laughed Tyler, running around and watching the

flames flickering along behind him. When they blew out, he looked temporarily disappointed. He concentrated hard, clenched his fists then gave a whoop of delight as his hands created fire again.

'Whoo hoo!' he cheered. 'This is awesome!'

'It's not awesome,' Rifle yelled in terror when he realised his own hands were alight. He tried to blow them out, but they flared into a giant wall of fire about four times his height.

'Whoa...' breathed Tyler in awe. Rifle screamed and dunked his arms into the river under the bridge. Finally, the fire disappeared.

'Can you teach me how to do that?' begged Tyler.

'N-no. I d-don't want that to ever h-happen again,' Rifle pulled his arms out of the water. He curled himself into a ball on the ground. He thought he heard a rustle in the bushes but didn't feel in the mood to check it out. Tyler played with his new fire power for a while before pausing.

'Did you hear that?' he whispered, sounding spooked.

'Hear what?' responded Rifle, wondering if Tyler heard the same rustle.

'Ooh, look. Who or what's that?' said Tyler, pointing into the shadows. Rifle reluctantly raised his head and spied a tall, athletic man almost hidden from view.

The man stepped into the light, revealing blond hair and a dark brown, skin-tight costume. He looked soaked through, which was no surprise considering the rain still pouring down behind him. A cat-like tail and ears attached to the costume made the twins doubt if he was even human.

'Don't be scared,' began the man, his voice a low growl. The twins could detect a subtle British accent.

'Dude, you're in a scary cat costume and a mask with glowing green eyes,' argued Tyler. 'What's not to be scared of?'

'You can call me Tiger-eye,' continued the man. 'I'm here to help. Do you have any place to stay?'

'No, our house burned down, and we think Mum and Dad have died,' replied Rifle miserably.

'I received an anonymous message that I would find you two here. The message told me that you were home-less and that I should take you to my house,' Tiger-eye still spoke in hushed tones.

'How do we know you're not just kidnapping us?' demanded Tyler loudly.

'Shhh, please keep it down,' cringed Tiger-eye, pulling out a piece of paper from his utility belt and showing it to the twins. 'Here's the note.'

To Tiger-Eye

They examined it carefully, then unanimously came to a conclusion.

'This was written by our brother, Kaine,' began Tyler.

'He makes the page like a grown-up's work and writes very perfectly,' nodded Rifle, pointing out the features on the note. 'Hey, you sound like a nice guy on this note.'

'Do you believe me yet?' prompted Tiger-eye. 'If even your brother's writing says it, how can you deny it?'

After a moment in thought, the twins entered a huddle.

'Do you think we should trust him?' whispered Rifle.

'We've got nowhere to go anyway,' replied Tyler. The twins turned to face Tiger-eye.

'Okay, we'll come,' they chorused.

Tiger-eye wordlessly scooped them up, one under each arm, and he re-entered the shadows.

'You'll need to be quiet,' he warned them, 'because we don't want people finding us. There are plenty of people who'd love to see me dead.'

The twins nodded to show they understood him, and the rest of the journey was made in silence. Rifle glanced at Tyler uncertainly, knitting his eyebrows together in concern. Who knew if they were doing the right thing by going with this man. Why would people want to see him dead? What had he done to them? Tyler shrugged carelessly in response. Despite the intimidating appearance and cryptic words of the man, something inside Rifle told him he could trust this stranger.

Settling In

Just before midnight, the trio arrived at an impressive mansion surrounded by huge Moreton Bay fig trees. Rifle gaped at the seven-storey, rectangular building and its intimidating cast iron front gates, which displayed the words 'Power Mansion' across the top.

'Boys, welcome to Power Mansion,' smiled Tiger-eye, setting the twins onto the ground.

'Where's Kaine?' demanded Rifle. 'I thought he'd be here.'

'I never told you he'd be here. I haven't even met the kid,' shrugged Tiger-eye. 'I wish I did know him, though. He could give me some answers as to why you're now in my custody.'

'What's custardy?' puzzled Tyler. 'Isn't that slimy and yellow and yummy and something on pudding?'

'No, it means I've got to look after you boys,' Tiger-eye

attempted to explain.

'Still don't get it. Why do *you* look after us?' Tyler pouted.

'Honestly, I don't know,' answered Tiger-eye. 'The message I received said you had no relatives apart from your brother. I don't get why your brother chose me.'

Although Rifle still didn't know whether to trust Tiger-eye, he longed to explore the impressive mansion. His exhaustion didn't quench his insatiable curiosity.

'Can we go inside?' begged Rifle.

'Yeah, can we?' added Tyler. 'It looks epic!'

'Sure, go ahead,' permitted Tiger-eye. 'My grandfather will let you in.'

They shot up the front stairs to the door, opened by an older, bearded gentleman in neat but casual clothes. The twins dashed past, barely glancing at him in their rush to explore the building. When they were safely inside, Tiger-eye nimbly climbed one of the huge Moreton Bay fig trees in the front yard.

Pulling a special branch, he activated an opening in the tree, jumping down the hole into the huge, cave-like storage room below. There, he discovered the clothes for his civilian identity out waiting for him.

Moments later, billionaire James Power emerged from

a large cupboard in the mansion's basement. He headed straight towards the old man while rubbing his hair dry with a towel.

'Grandfather, how are the boys going?' he asked.

'They seem to enjoy finding out how many rooms are in the building,' replied Grandfather. 'The one in the red shirt doesn't seem in the least bit worried about all the changes, but the one in the blue shirt seems very... unsettled, to say the least.'

'According to the note, Tyler wears red and Rifle wears blue,' reminded James. He glanced down at his watch, which scanned through the security cameras, and found that the twins had reached the music room. James jogged to meet them, and he arrived just as Tyler picked up an electric guitar and began viciously strumming tuneless chords. He cleared his throat to try and get Tyler's attention, but Tyler was so preoccupied making clashy noises he didn't hear him.

'Tyler, please,' started James, raising his voice and muting the guitar strings with his fingers.

'Who are you, and how do you know my name?' demanded Tyler.

'I'm James, but you would know me as Tiger-eye,' he answered calmly, lifting the guitar out of Tyler's grasp. Tyler shrugged and ran off across the deep red carpet. James watched for a moment to make sure Tyler stayed in the same room, and when satisfied, he turned back to Rifle.

'So, you're the guy who took us here,' stated Rifle half-questioningly. He sat quietly on the piano stool, hands resting lightly on the piano keys.

'Yes, but don't tell anyone. It's a secret.'

'Why didn't you come to us looking normal?'

'You wouldn't understand,' James almost didn't continue but then added, 'I can't be seen on the streets at night like this. To criminals, I look more vulnerable than when I'm dressed as Tiger-eye.'

'Oh,' Rifle didn't truly understand, but he didn't press for a better explanation, turning back to the piano.

He played a haunting, sad tune by pressing one finger on each key, and he repeated it over and over until James spoke.

'Rifle, if you keep playing that, you're going to make me cry,' James joked. 'It's so sad.'

'Ooh, okay.' Rifle played the tune again with a faint smirk. 'Let's see the tears.'

'Cheeky scoundrel,' laughed James, pulling Rifle's hands away and shutting the piano.

Tyler began bashing the drum set, putting his heart and soul into making the most chaotic sounds possible.

'Tyler!' yelled James, snatching him off the drum set stool. At a more usual volume, James continued, 'It's one o'clock in the morning, so that's way too loud.'

'Aw, you're just ruining all my fun.' Tyler scowled, sticking out his bottom lip.

'I think we'll head to the bedrooms now. You guys can choose your bedrooms in the hallway on the third storey.' James led the twins to the nearest elevator. 'And if you're hungry, then I can get you something to eat. I'm afraid I don't have any clothes your size, so you're going to have to keep using the ones you have on you.' He wrinkled his nose at the smoky smell and dirt caked into the twins' clothes and hair. He decided they would have a bath and a shopping trip in the morning.

While the twins chose their bedrooms, James slid his back down the wall, running his hands through his hair.

'What have I got myself into?'

Getting to Know the Twins

The next morning, at the breakfast table, James asked the twins about themselves.

'I like to annoy people,' grinned Tyler, tugging Rifle's hair persistently.

'You don't need to demonstrate,' replied James hastily, seeing Rifle's irritated face.

'I like sword fighting,' commented Rifle shyly, blushing when Tyler laughed.

'That's a stupid hobby. When are you ever gonna use that in life?' ridiculed Tyler.

'Tyler,' frowned James warningly. 'Enough.' Tyler sulkily fell silent, and Rifle stirred his cereal.

'Are you going to eat that?' asked James kindly.

'I'm not hungry,' sighed Rifle.

'I'll eat it,' offered Tyler, taking Rifle's bowl and eating from it. 'Yummy!'

James stood up and walked over to Rifle's chair. He rested a hand on the troubled boy's shoulder, before motioning to the door and leading him out of the room.

'So,' began James, 'tell me about this sword fighting hobby of yours. I'm quite fond of the art myself, though I don't do it often.'

'I've been learning since I could walk, but I still can't use a full-size sword. Something about me being too short or something,' responded Rifle. A look of determination crossed his face. 'As soon as I grow enough to use a full-size sword, I'm gonna be the best swordsman ever.'

'I'm sure you will,' encouraged James. 'Now let's see those skills.'

'Okay,' nodded Rifle, looking much happier.

*　　*　　*

James watched as Rifle demonstrated his sword fighting abilities. The moves were complicated for someone so young, but the technique tended to be imprecise and sloppy.

'Very good,' applauded James when Rifle came over for a sip of water. 'We'll work on improving that as soon as you're ready.'

'Now,' bounced Rifle. 'I'm ready now.'

'Really? All right then,' smiled James, standing up and grasping a sword of his own. He began to correct Rifle's technique, pleased with how well the six-year-old responded so readily.

'This is dumb,' complained Tyler, appearing at the doorway to the gym.

'Tyler,' said James, struggling to sound patient. 'There is nothing wrong with Rifle's hobby. He's going great with it.'

'I'll show you great,' backchatted Tyler, his hands sprouting flames. 'Being able to do *this* is great.'

'Put it away, Tyler,' begged Rifle, stepping back from his brother. Sparks flew from his own hands and a fire ignited on each finger. He cried out fearfully, accidentally causing the flames to flare higher.

'Ooh! Ooh! Make it even bigger!' exclaimed Tyler, extinguishing his own fire to watch Rifle's.

'No. I can't control it!' yelled the terrified Rifle.

James, who'd incredulously watched the events unfold, realised he needed to step in before things went terribly wrong. He had no idea how the twins were creating fire with their hands, but he'd heard of similar superpowers before.

'Calm down, Rifle,' soothed James. 'It's okay, none of the equipment in here will catch alight. Try taking some deep breaths.'

As Rifle tried to calm down, the fire gave one last flare before flickering out.

'Well done. You did it,' congratulated James warmly. 'No damage done either. But how could you do that? The fire from your hands?' Rifle shrugged with eyes cast to the floor. James studied his face for a moment. 'You haven't had this power for long, have you?'

Rifle nodded in confirmation. James could tell Rifle had withdrawn into his shell, and there wouldn't be any more sword fighting with him that day. He turned to Tyler.

'Now you, young man, are in big trouble,' he scolded, taking Tyler by the ear and dragging him out of the gym. 'What were you even thinking? You're grounded.'

'How long?' Tyler crossed his arms and glared up at James defiantly as they marched.

'You'll stay in your room and think about the consequences of your actions until dinnertime,' sentenced James, releasing Tyler in the bedroom. 'Grandfather will bring you your meals.'

He shut the door and breathed a heavy sigh. *Two kids with fiery superpowers... How will I manage?* he thought to himself as he walked away. His new responsibility to look after the now homeless and orphaned twins wasn't something he'd expected or had time to prepare for, and he still wondered why he, of all people, had been chosen as their guardian.

New Home

A few weeks passed, and there was still no sign of the twins' parents. Rifle stayed in his room unless James insisted he come out for food. Even then, Rifle hardly ate.

'I miss Mum and Dad,' sighed Rifle, pushing a potato around his plate with a fork. 'Do you miss them too?'

Tyler shrugged but dipped his eyes to hide the tears suddenly appearing. He shoved so much food in his mouth that it would be impossible to speak. James walked in at that moment.

'Tyler, that was too much,' scolded James. 'Yuck, no, don't spit it out! That's disgusting. Just swallow your mouthful and don't put that much in next time.' Tyler rolled his eyes with more attitude than should belong to a six-year-old, but he did obey.

'What's gonna happen to us if Mum and Dad never show up?' Rifle stared at James with big, miserable eyes.

'Uh… various options,' he answered, caught off guard for a moment. 'Either I adopt you, or you end up at an orphanage to be adopted by someone else.'

'Orphanage?' gasped Rifle, nightmarish images of an evil orphanage owner and flashing lightning above an ominous prison coming to mind. 'No, I'm not going to an orphanage! Never!'

'It's your choice. I'm happy to adopt you if you would like,' reassured James. When Rifle opened his mouth to speak, James held up his hands. 'You don't have to decide now. There's plenty of time for that later.' Rifle closed his mouth and nodded.

'You gonna eat that potato?' questioned Tyler. 'If not, I'll eat it.' Rifle pushed his plate toward Tyler.

'Just one question… What's adopt?' Rifle tilted his head to one side.

'It means I become your official guardian, or new dad if you prefer,' explained James. 'And by the way, I know I'd never replace your real dad. I don't intend to.' He patted Rifle on the shoulder as he stood up. 'I just want you guys to be happy.' James didn't want history to repeat itself. Not while he could help it.

'Are you normal kids?' asked James as he tucked Rifle

into bed. 'As in, do you like bedtime stories?'

'Yes,' replied Rifle, a 'duh' tone in his voice. 'Mum reads… used to read to us every night.'

'All right…' James pulled a picture frame off the wall, one with a photo of a ship on water. From behind it, he took out a book with a bright, colourful cover. 'I have this book called 'The Seasick Pirate'. Interested in hearing it?'

'Yeah!' exclaimed Rifle, and Tyler shot out from his own room to listen.

Rifle marvelled at the fact that the book had come from a picture frame. There were a huge number of frames around the mansion, and he briefly wondered how many others were hiding things behind them. But he kept his questions to himself.

James climbed onto the bed, and the twins sat on either side of him. As James began to read, Rifle stared at the man in admiration. His British voice could change drastically to become just like a pirate's snarl, and his voice for the pirate's mother had the twins in fits of laughter. James had a hard time not laughing along with them.

When the story ended, James brought Tyler back to bed. Then, he returned to Rifle.

'If my parents don't show up, I'm definitely staying with

THE SEASILK PIRATE

you,' commented Rifle sleepily, yawning. 'You're fun.'

'I'm glad to hear that,' smiled James. 'Goodnight, Rifle.'

'G'night, New Dad,' replied Rifle. James paused at the doorway, realising from Rifle's short conversation that the boy had decided for himself that his parents might not be coming back.

Chapter 7

At the Hospital

A light-blue clad nurse walked up to Dr Tener, holding a clipboard.

'How's our burns patient going?' asked Dr Tener.

'His injuries are healing incredibly well, considering it's only been a couple of weeks,' reported the nurse. 'But he's still suffering.'

'From the burns?'

'No. Come and see for yourself,' the nurse led Dr Tener to the patient's room in the day ward. Dr Tener peeked through the curtains to find the bandaged and scruffy patient staring at the roof.

'It's my fault,' he whispered hoarsely. 'They're all dead... because of me.' Seeming to notice Dr Tener there, he raised his voice. 'I should've listened! Then none of this would've happened.' Tears ran down his ragged, haunted face, and he shuddered. 'Amelia,' he barely spoke above a whisper,

suddenly giving a loud, anguished cry that made his smoke-damaged voice crack. 'Amelia!! Why did this have to happen?!'

'We've had to sedate him at night so that the other patients can sleep,' explained the nurse. 'He just keeps going on like that, and we can't get any sense out of him... his name, age, family members...'

'Poor man. What happened to him again?' Dr Tener adjusted his black-framed glasses, which had the annoying habit of sliding down the bridge of his nose.

'According to the paramedics and fire crew, there was a fire in the family home, and only this man was rescued,' answered the nurse, consulting her notes. 'The fire brigade said the fire got out of control really fast, and there was nothing he could've done to save the others anyway.'

Dr Tener glanced at the guilt-ridden man, and he felt there was more to the story than that.

Adoption

Tyler didn't ease up on teasing and harassing Rifle, to James' dismay. The man didn't like sending Tyler to his room all the time, but he didn't know how else to deal with the troublesome six-year-old.

'They're not my kids! I don't know the first thing about disciplining them,' he complained to Grandfather.

'You'll manage. They look up to you.'

In his spare time when the twins were occupied watching movies, James searched tirelessly for any trace of the twins' parents, brother or relations. All he found was a missing person's report stating that Jason, Amelia and Kaine Young hadn't been seen since the fire that destroyed their home. Thanks to the fact that James told the police the whereabouts of the twins, Rifle and Tyler were not on that list.

James eventually discovered a promising website that listed the names he was searching for. Immediately, he clicked on the link, but it led him to an error page.

'This page could not be displayed. It may have been moved or deleted,' read out James. He buried his face in his hands and groaned, 'Oh come on. This shouldn't be so difficult. It's almost as though every useful record of the family has been removed!'

Rifle marched into the room angrily, and Tyler followed close behind. Both started yelling over the top of each other, so James couldn't hear a word either of them was trying to say.

'Guys, one at a time,' hushed James. 'Rifle, what's wrong?'

'Tyler said we'd never see our parents again,' Rifle's voice was higher with fury.

'Cuz it's true! They're dead!' insisted Tyler.

'And I told him that they might've got out of the house in time,' continued Rifle.

'I said they couldn't. They're all burnt to crisps and deaded,' scowled Tyler.

'Don't speak like that,' scolded James. 'It's entirely unnecessary and obviously upsetting your brother.'

'That's what *I* told him, and he bit me,' Rifle held up his hand to display the row of pink marks. 'Then I did the fire thing, not on purpose, and burnt the roof.'

'Which room?' James stood, wondering if the ceiling was still on fire. He didn't want a repeat of the twins' home scenario.

'The TV room, I think… or maybe it was the cinema or the theatre,' frowned Rifle. 'I can't remember which one, there are so many rooms here.'

'Let's go and check out the room you just came from now.'

Tyler, eager to get Rifle in trouble, quickly showed James to the room with black scorch marks covering the furniture and ceiling. Tyler waited for the scolding to come; he would certainly be told off if *he* burnt the room like that. But James didn't yell, and he didn't send Rifle to his bedroom. To Tyler's dismay, James placed a comforting hand on Rifle's shoulder.

'It's okay. Accidents happen. This is only surface damage. Thank goodness nothing actually caught alight. Those black marks? They'll wash off with some scrubbing.'

Tyler ran off, poking his tongue at Rifle spitefully. Rifle didn't understand why his brother was being so mean but decided to ignore it.

'Rifle, I wanted to tell you something.' James crouched to match his height with Rifle's. 'I've been searching for your parents and your brother…'

'Uh-huh?' Rifle nodded, the hope in his eyes paining James.

'I'm really sorry, but I can't find any traces of them at all.' Rifle's face crumbled.

'You don't think I'll ever see them again?' he asked in a small voice.

'I'm not saying it's impossible, but it's... not looking good,' answered James quietly.

'But... Mum and Dad...' Rifle bravely held back his tears

for a few moments before breaking into inconsolable sobs. 'Why did this happen?'

James stroked Rifle's hair and allowed the distraught boy to cry on his shoulder.

'It'll be okay,' whispered James, sure that the young boy wouldn't actually hear over the sobbing. 'The pain will fade. It always does... eventually.'

Runaway

Dr Tener moved around to every patient, checking their progress and making notes. All patients but one had been accounted for and were recovering nicely; so far, so good. He still needed to check on his most puzzling patient, and this particular one weighed heavily on the doctor's mind.

The nameless man had recently been given plastic surgery, hopefully restoring his partially disfigured face to its usual appearance, but the surgeons had no idea what he'd looked like before. The innovative technology and techniques used could guarantee hair regrowth and no scars, so Dr Tener wasn't concerned about the patient's physical injuries.

The patient's mind seemed to be in an endless loop of grief, blame, guilt and mental agony, problems that the doctors and nurses weren't trained to deal with at this hospital. After surgery, the patient had stopped calling out and making such a fuss, only to enter an impenetrable silence that rendered him unresponsive and decidedly difficult to work with.

Dr Tener snapped out of his thoughts, and taking a deep breath, he entered the patient's homely room. He dropped his arms by his side in dismay.

The bed and linen cupboard were devoid of sheets, and the patient wasn't anywhere in sight. Dr Tener hurried over to stare out the open window. He could only assume that, just like in so many movies, the patient had tied sheets together and escaped out the window, which was now missing flywire. The trail of sheets still dangled from the windowsill, and the patient had left the flywire on the ground nearby with a pile of bandages that should have been on his burns.

'Maggie, he's gone,' Dr Tener raised his voice enough that the passing nurse could hear.

'The mystery patient?' gaped Maggie, stopping in her tracks.

'Yes. How long has he been left alone at one time?' He adjusted his glasses; the more agitated he became, the more often they fell off his nose.

'Um, I'm not sure, but no more than an hour...'

'Well, it's obviously been long enough for him to tie twenty-odd sheets together and climb out the window.'

'It was Sharon's shift last. I just got here,' justified Maggie, lifting her hands blamelessly. She hurried away to complete her tasks.

'Who knows how long he's been gone,' huffed Dr Tener, correcting his glasses yet again. 'Now, he could be anywhere.' He immediately told the receptionist to call the police to begin a search for the missing man.

Training Begins

With Rifle and Tyler's consent, James adopted them both on the condition that if their real parents were found, they could return to them. When the adoption process was complete, the boys began to settle into their new life.

While Tyler appeared like he couldn't care less about what happened with the fire that destroyed his home, Rifle was traumatised. James found that the boy suffered from frequent nightmares, waking up in a cold sweat then silently crying himself to sleep again.

It nearly broke James' heart knowing the turmoil that raged inside someone so young, but he didn't know if he could do anything to help.

Each day, James worked with Rifle to help him learn to control his powers by controlling his emotions. Rifle, although still terrified of fire, began to realise the potential of the superpower and became less reluctant to activate it when James instructed him to use it.

Soon, Rifle filled his spare time with sword fighting lessons with James, staying active to drive negative thoughts out of his head.

Tyler tended to stay in his room, playing video games whenever anyone watched him, but when he was alone, he worked on a cape, which would turn its wearer invisible. He intended for the cape to help him play pranks on Rifle undiscovered, but he lacked the knowledge to build it correctly. He just played pranks without invisibility instead.

As years passed, Rifle's nightmares became less frequent, and control over his powers grew. His sword fighting skills surpassed James', so he took classes elsewhere to continue to improve. To make sure Rifle possessed all-round abilities, James also taught him martial arts.

School hindered Rifle's progress on weekdays, and he would make up for lost time over weekends. Tyler couldn't believe that Rifle would waste so much time and energy on doing all the 'active stuff', as he called it.

On Rifle's eleventh birthday, he approached James with a serious request.

'Dad, make me a superhero. Please.'

James couldn't help but feel chuffed whenever Rifle

SPARBOT
MEDIUM
For teens and small adults

called him 'Dad', which only recently began happening. Rifle had dropped the nickname of 'New Dad' in favour of just 'Dad'. Tyler still just called him 'James', not out of respect for his own parents, but out of spite.

'Rifle, it's a big thing you're asking. Your physical training will need to increase tenfold, and your mind, as smart as it already is, will need to be sharpened further. Your powers must be completely under control, no unexpected flares or flickers.'

Rifle swallowed hard but nodded.

'Yes, I'd do that.'

'Just out of interest, why are you so keen on this idea?' asked James.

'Well…' Rifle gave a mischievous grin, 'I'd love to prove to Tyler that sword fighting isn't dumb.' He became serious as he continued, 'I want to stop bad things from happening to others. I know I couldn't have done anything for my parents, but maybe I could save others' lives if I was a superhero.'

'A very noble reason,' agreed James. 'Well, if you're ready for your life to change forever, let's start this insane training.'

'Oh yeah. Let's do this!'

Training Continues

The next few weeks were the most challenging Rifle had ever experienced. James wasn't kidding about anything he'd told him. The tween still needed to complete school amongst his far more difficult training regime, and on top of that, he also spent half the night studying criminal psychology each night. By the end of only the first week, he was exhausted.

As James watched him sleeping, flaked out over his criminal studies, James thought how much Rifle must've desired to be a superhero. Not once had he complained about late nights with lack of sleep, James' almost unfairly strict behaviour or the amount of time spent working on complete mastery of his powers.

'Sorry buddy,' murmured James, moving over to him and placing a hand on his shoulder to wake him gently. 'You'll need to be awake and ready for school.'

Rifle sleepily lifted his head, rubbing his eyes groggily.

'I didn't finish reading Chapter 103 last night...' he apologised hoarsely. His head dropped to the table with a bang that startled him awake, and he stood up.

'Okay, I'm awake,' reassured Rifle, staggering over to his school uniform. When he finished dressing himself and getting ready for school, James dropped him off in front of the school.

'Good luck in school today, hey?' smiled James as Rifle grabbed his backpack from the boot of the car. 'Try not to fall asleep in class.'

'I'll try,' promised Rifle, dragging himself and his backpack to the school building.

Tyler, full of energy, ran ahead of him, sticking out his tongue and blowing a raspberry.

'Brothers,' sighed Rifle with a shake of his head.

*　　*　　*

At the end of the day, James brought the twins aside.

'Rifle, Tyler tells me that today, you punched him during lunch break,' began James.

'He told me I was useless at everything and that if I fell

asleep for the rest of the day, it wouldn't change my grades at all,' protested Rifle. 'And he wouldn't leave me alone when I told him to.'

'I was only joking about the grades thing,' sulked Tyler, applying soothing cream to the dark, puffy circle around one eye. 'You're so on edge. I thought it was funny.'

'Well, it obviously wasn't for Rifle,' replied James. 'Tyler, you're grounded from video games until tomorrow evening.'

'But I was the one who got hurt,' pouted Tyler, fake tears flowing easily from his eyes as he ran off. 'It's not fair!'

James rolled his eyes and turned to Rifle, ignoring Tyler's outburst.

'Now, Rifle, I know you're tired, which makes you irritable, but it's no excuse for punching anyone.'

'Yeah,' sighed Rifle, lowering his gaze remorsefully. 'Sorry.'

'I'll have to punish you too, but I think it will be a relief for you. I'm banning you from training for three days.'

Rifle couldn't be sure if he felt disappointed that he could no longer train, or if he were pleased about the chance to catch up on sleep. As soon as James dismissed him, he headed up to his room and got into bed, not even caring that he would miss dinner. He drifted into a dream-filled sleep.

X-FILES
BAK PAK
SHARP-NR

Rifle walked along a busy street, following a tall, unkempt man in ragged clothes. When he called out to him, the man turned around slowly, revealing the face of his father, Jason. Jason stared without any recognition in his eyes, and he attempted to remind his father of who he was. The blank expression didn't change as Jason turned away, ignoring his pleas to come back.

Rifle woke up in the middle of the night, heart beating quickly. He wiped his clammy palms across his moist forehead, trying to remove the image of emotionless Jason from his head.

He'd had that dream before, too many times. It left him with the feeling that his father was alive but that there was something very wrong. Had his father forgotten him? It hurt him to think of the very possibility. He wished he could find out for real, but he secretly feared the truth. If his nightmare showed him what his father had truly become, he would rather he'd never found out.

Rifle sighed, afraid to close his eyes in case the images returned, but soon, his exhaustion forced him back to sleep.

*   *   *

Over the next couple of days, his tiredness got the better of him, and he couldn't help but sleep, despite fears of nightmares. When he woke up, he felt much brighter and ready to train again. He coped better with the lack of sleep this time, so his training lasted for a month. After a few nights off, he felt ready to train again.

With each break, his endurance levels rose, and he could achieve greater goals. As more and more months passed, James felt more ready for Rifle to join him on the streets to fight crime.

Chapter 12

The Test

First, there would be a test to find out if Rifle's abilities were enough. James didn't tell him when the test would occur but waited until the boy turned thirteen. Then, he inconspicuously examined his training and gave him challenges he needed to complete.

'Create a clone of yourself out of fire,' instructed James.

Rifle obeyed, creating a fiery-coloured lookalike that held his hand where the fire needed to be in contact with his skin.

'Now turn that clone into a ball and throw it at that wall.'

The clone morphed into a fireball the size of Rifle's head, and he catapulted it at the sturdy, already scorch-marked wall.

James took Rifle to a specific place in the training room and pointed out the next challenge.

'Okay, there's a group of criminals past that wall,' he

began, showing Rifle a wall three times James' height. 'They've stolen a fragile jewel. This.' James held up a fake gem made of glass. 'They've seen you coming and are starting to throw the jewel to each other to make it more difficult for you to get it. You must intercept their passes without breaking the jewel.'

When Rifle nodded, James moved over to a group of sparring robots, called Sparbots, and handed them the fake gem. The Sparbots headed to specified locations and began throwing the gem to each other.

Rifle stepped back to provide space for a run-up, then he used the momentum of his sprint to launch himself up the wall. Once he reached the top, he crouched down, calculating his next move carefully. As one robot threw the gem into the air, Rifle pushed himself off the wall, hands outstretched. He caught the gem and landed in a roll, his body cushioning the impact.

Then, the robots turned toward him and began to attack!

'Hey! You never said this was part of the challenge,' yelped Rifle, dodging punches from the Sparbots.

'I never said it wasn't,' smiled James. 'You need to expect the unexpected.'

As Rifle dodged attacks, he assessed the situation. There

were six of the enemy. He couldn't 'hurt' the Sparbots because that would oppose James' rule of not injuring anyone unless they endangered him first. He only used evasive manoeuvres to get out of the Sparbots' reach and handed the gem to James.

'If I had some kind of rope, I'd tie these guys up, but I don't have anything,' Rifle told him. 'With these particular criminals, I could shut them down, but most other criminals don't have that function.' A cheeky grin crossed his face as he re-entered

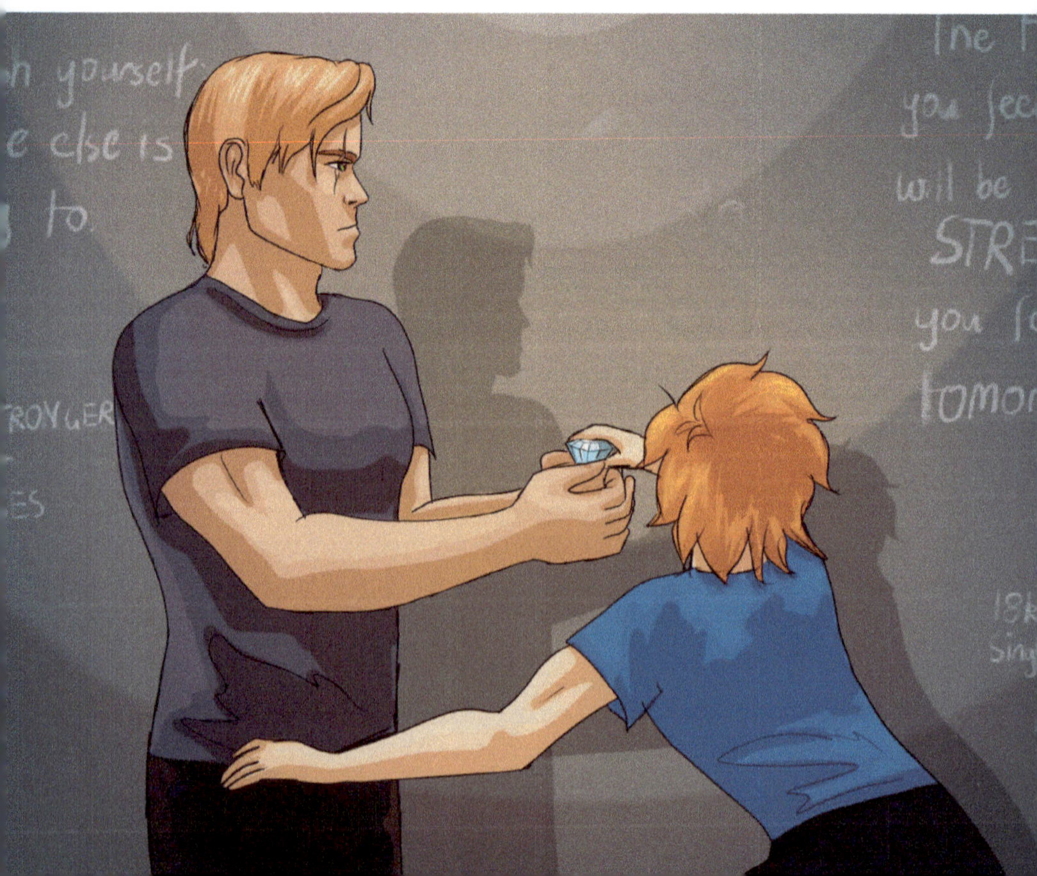

the battle. Rifle dropped a pellet in front of the Sparbots, and the pellet exploded into a smokescreen with chloroform gas.

He held his breath as he crawled away from the area.

The Sparbots detected chloroform in the air and acted accordingly: falling to the ground as if asleep.

'All right, where did you get that from?' asked James, once they were a safe distance from the gas.

'From your utility belt under your shirt. I took it when I handed you the jewel.'

'Oh, you sneaky pick-pocket,' smirked James, annoyed he hadn't noticed it but impressed with Rifle's ability to take something out from under his nose so unnoticeably.

After more challenges, James told Rifle to wear a blindfold.

'You will dodge attacks from this Sparbot, sword fighting style. Do not peek through the blindfold; this is a test for your other senses.'

A fierce duel began, and Rifle struggled to fight the robot, without possessing vision.

'I can't do this!' yelled Rifle.

'Listen for the sound of the Sparbot's motors, the swish of the sword. Feel the disturbance in the airflow of the room. These will give you clues to the next move.'

PART 1
Warm ups -
PART
Cardio
SPARBOT
PRO
SPARBOT
PRO

When Rifle calmed down, he realised he could hear where the robot's sword was headed and moved away from that area. He continued to easily dodge attacks until James told him to stop.

'Let's give it a break for a minute. Have a drink of water, some food,' suggested James, leading Rifle out of the training room to the bench seats just outside. Rifle was momentarily distracted by the fitness poster on the wall there. He hadn't noticed before just how similar James' physique was to the model in the poster, and he decided it was quite impressive.

'I just wanted to tell you something... about me.' James sat down, prompting Rifle to do the same, and Rifle's ears perked up. James hardly ever talked about himself.

'I'm blind in my right eye,' continued James, pointing to a faint scar that ran down one eye. The eye itself hardly seemed different to his left eye. 'I used to long to be a superhero and trained as hard as you, but then this happened.'

'What happened?' asked Rifle eagerly.

'A tiger escaped from a zoo and attacked many people... including me.'

'Whoa,' breathed Rifle. He suddenly understood why it

had been so easy to take the gas pellet from James. He'd kept his arm out of James' vision purely by chance, not having any idea he was taking advantage of James' partial blindness.

'Some of the other people received serious injuries, but they all healed up without a problem. Because of my new blindness, I thought my crimefighting career was over before it even began. That is, until my long-lost grandfather showed up. I'd been living on my own before then and training solo, but Grandfather began teaching me new techniques and how to fight without any vision whatsoever. It meant I could easily fight with only one eye to assist me.'

'Huh,' nodded Rifle. Then, realisation hit. 'Oh, you're blind-folding me to make sure I'm even better than before!'

'Yep,' confirmed James. He thought about telling Rifle about a time when he had neither vision nor hearing, but he decided that would be a story for another time. He stood up. 'By the way, you've passed the test. I'll work on the blindfold training with you, but for now, you're ready to come with me to fight crime.'

'That was the test?! I passed the test?' gaped Rifle incredulously. 'I can't believe it!'

'Well, you'd better believe it,' smiled James. 'Next up, we'll make your costume.'

'Cool!' exclaimed Rifle. 'I've got this design where it's blue, with like a black cape, gloves and boots. There'll be a symbol of two swords crossed on the chest, and I'll have a utility belt with...'

'Slow down,' laughed James. 'You can make the costume look however you like as long as it contains certain features: Fire-proof so you don't burn your costume every time you use your power, shock-absorbent, tear-resistant material.'

'All right,' agreed Rifle, nearly bouncing out of his skin.

Over the next few weeks, James and Rifle worked together to build the costume. While James took care of the technical details, Rifle worked on the design. Soon, they finished the costume and Rifle wore it fully for the first time.

He stared at himself in the mirror in awe.

'It's so great! It's just how I hoped it would be.'

'Good. Tonight, you'll be trying it out on the streets of this city,' replied James, 'under the supervision of Tiger-eye.'

When night-time arrived, James became Tiger-eye. After Rifle dressed in his superhero costume too, Tiger-eye smiled at him and asked,

'Are you ready, 'Master of Swords'?'

'Yes, Tiger-eye. I am.'

Tyler glared jealously at the pair as they left. He wanted a

costume too, and he didn't think it was fair that Rifle got nearly James' full attention. All Tyler received was a greeting in the morning, and a goodnight in the evening before James would rush off to help Rifle train.

Maybe if Tyler proved how great he was without training, James would pay more attention to him. Tyler schemed a way of doing just that, and the first step was to steal the designs for his brother's costume. He would show James that he could use the plans to make his own costume without the help that Rifle had needed.

Tyler stared down at a small slip of paper he always kept in his pocket: a job advertisement for a very interesting position. The job description stated requirements for complete secrecy and the ability to follow orders. Tyler knew he could do both, and he realised this would prove to James just how awesome and capable he could be... if James ever found out.

APPLY NOW!

First Night

Tiger-eye and Rifle travelled on foot to the centre of the Umbre City. As they walked, Rifle spoke quietly.

'I'm thinking I'll call myself Sword Master, you know, to match the symbol on the costume and my sword fighting abilities. Also, what you called me earlier: Master of Swords. I think it sounds better like Sword Master.'

'Sure, Sword Master,' Tiger-eye rolled his eyes good-naturedly, feeling a little relieved when Sword Master stopped talking. He liked to walk in silence, listening for what his eyes couldn't detect.

'Ooh, look... there's a guy up to no good! See? See?' whispered Sword Master excitedly, pointing to a dark-clad man carrying a sack over his shoulder. 'Gotta stop him from getting away with those stolen goods!' Tiger-eye grasped Sword Master's cape to prevent him from running there.

'Not so fast. That's Rob Peterson, a police officer. He does late-night shopping,' pointed out Tiger-eye. 'Those 'stolen goods' are his groceries.' Sword Master could just make out the police uniform in the semi-darkness, and he sighed.

'I still have so-o-o much to learn.'

Rob glanced over to them and gave a cheery wave, and Tiger-eye saluted back while Sword Master hesitantly waved.

'He's one of the nicer guys in the police force. More tolerant to vigilantes,' explained Tiger-eye when Rob was out of earshot.

'Oh boy. What a mistake I could've made.' Sword Master hung his head in shame.

'Don't dwell on it. Everyone makes mistakes,' responded Tiger-eye, continuing to walk on. Soon, the vigilantes came across the first real crime that night.

'Gimme all yer valuables,' demanded the thief, holding a gun at a terrified couple, who began taking out their wallets.

Tiger-eye nudged Sword Master, encouraging him to stop the man. Sword Master silently sprinted behind the criminal, sneaking up and slapping the weapon out of the man's hands. The man yelled in shock, whipping around to face the thirteen-year-old.

'Aw, look, it's a cute little boy,' taunted the criminal, 'in his daddy's cosplay. Whatcha gonna do? Pull out a toy gun and shoot me with foam bullets?'

Sword Master glared out from under his reddish-orange fringe, then he raised his hands. Flames shot out of his fingertips, blazing around the thief like a burning cage. The couple ran away, taking the opportunity to escape.

'Where didja get that from?' wondered the criminal, trembling as the fire died down.

'My 'daddy's cosplay', obviously,' shrugged Sword Master

sarcastically. He found a pair of handcuffs in his utility belt and snapped them on the thief's wrists. The thief was too scared to resist.

Tiger-eye moved out of the shadows, activating a tracking device to let the police know a criminal needed to be arrested. He placed the device next to the thief, whose eyes widened.

'Y-you were with him?' gaped the man, turning pale. He immediately fainted.

'Wow, criminals really are terrified of you,' marvelled Sword Master. Tiger-eye nodded.

'They've all heard of me as a myth, an invincible creature that avenges wrongs.'

'How much is true?' asked Sword Master curiously, and they continued walking on.

'I'm not just a myth, but I do avenge wrongs. The invincible part is half-true. When criminals injure me, it sure would seem like I'm not hurt, but it's just delayed responses to pain and poisonous substances, thanks to special training of my mind. I can trick my body into thinking there's nothing wrong for a little while.'

'Huh, that's kind of like a superpower in itself,' grinned Sword Master. 'Impressive. You'll have to teach me sometime.' He paused a moment, staring into the shadows. 'I... just want to check something out,' he whispered, raising one hand in a fist. 'I thought I just saw someone walking around in black clothes. Don't worry, I won't attack straight away. I just need to make sure the person isn't up to anything.'

'I'll watch from here, just in case.'

Sword Master sprinted toward the suspicious activity, his rubber-soled boots making no sound on the sidewalk. He turned into an alleyway in time to witness a female figure entering a rundown old apartment.

The lady owned keys to the door, but nothing about

how she moved spelled someone coming home from late-night shopping. She closed the door behind her, locking it, and Sword Master moved closer. He found a small window to one side of the door, which he could see through by standing on his tiptoes.

Sword Master watched as the lady, who seemed to be in her mid-thirties, approached a young teenage boy.

Both stood in the darkened room, with a dim light bulb hanging from the ceiling. The lady's face was hidden by a mask and shadowed by a thick curtain of dark brown hair.

'I came as you asked,' began the lady.

'Good. I have a new task for you tonight,' spoke the boy. He handed the lady a gun-shaped weapon. 'This frequency ray needs testing, and there are two superheroes out in the city tonight who would be perfect test subjects...'

'Yes sir,' saluted the lady, accepting the weapon and vanishing into the shadows.

Sword Master pulled away from the building quickly and tore out toward Tiger-eye.

'Tiger-eye! I need to tell you something... urgently,' he panted, more from fear than from exertion.

Suddenly, a high-pitched tone tore through the air, making the vigilantes' ears ache. They covered their ears quickly, but the sound penetrated their hands and still entered their heads, making their brains feel fuzzy.

'Make it stop!' yelled Sword Master, dropping to his knees. 'Stop!' He curled himself into a ball to try to block out the sound, which seemed to be increasing in volume by the second.

The lady approached them, wearing all black and a

domino mask, and she held a frequency ray at them. The weapon was capable of emitting pitches from ultrasonic to infrasonic, and it was currently set on the most painful pitch for human ears.

'Why are you... doing this?' Tiger-eye managed to ask her.

'Just testing out a weapon for my boss. I'd say it works perfectly,' smirked the lady smugly, walking away and vanishing from sight. Gradually, the sound faded away too.

'My brain hurts,' moaned Sword Master, forcing himself to stand up.

'Mine too,' replied Tiger-eye softly. 'My ears are still ringing. But I'm wondering who her boss is... Why would this person be making weapons like that?' He slapped his ears gently to try and clear the buzzing, but to no avail. 'This'll probably clear after a while.' Sword Master stuck his fingers into his ears as if trying to pull the sound out.

'So that's it? The lady comes, makes our brains hurt, then she just leaves?' he scowled, crossing his arms. 'I saw them planning it, her and the boy. But how do we find out what they're scheming?'

'I... there's usually methods, but it's so... difficult to

think,' muttered Tiger-eye, rubbing the back of his head in confusion.

The lady watched, hidden in the darkness and writing notes on her observations. She smiled to herself, beginning a silent jog away from the shadows.

'Let's play a little game of cat-and-mouse,' she murmured, deliberately moving into the light just enough for the superheroes to notice her.

'There she is!' yelped Sword Master, shooting off after her.

As Tiger-eye began to run too, he heard a frantic cry that sounded like a mother calling her child. Due to his ringing ears, he could hardly hear the child's name or from where the voice was coming, but he methodically followed the sound and found the mother. She told him that her son had run off and now she couldn't find him.

'He's only two,' explained the mother tearfully. Tiger-eye nodded before climbing a skyscraper to get a better view of his surroundings, and he held an electronic magnification lens up to his good eye. He scanned the city streets systematically until he noticed a young boy wandering out onto a road.

Tiger-eye leaped off the skyscraper to a lower building,

then a lower one again before finally landing on the ground near the road. He approached the child, who seemed to be examining a snail crossing the road.

'Hey, kid,' whispered Tiger-eye. 'I think it's a good idea if you get off the road.' He glanced around, hoping traffic wouldn't arrive before he'd convinced the child to move. The child seemed to ignore him, so he tried again.

'Hello? Earth to little boy,' He waved a hand in front of the child's face. 'You're kind of in danger here.'

When the boy didn't respond again, Tiger-eye attempted to lift him up, but the boy scurried just out of reach and bent down to pick up a stone.

Meanwhile, Sword Master pulled out a tranquilliser blowgun as he sprinted after the frequency ray lady. She was surprisingly fast and agile, making it a challenge just for Sword Master to keep up with her. He shot some darts at her, missing her by mere millimetres.

Then, she made an error that became her downfall. She looked back and laughed. That move slowed her down enough that Sword Master finally succeeded in hitting her with a dart. The lady stopped running and plucked the dart off her, throwing it away. Her dark eyes stared at Sword Master as if challenging him, then she collapsed.

He grabbed her arms and hoisted them over his shoulder, dragging her behind him to return to Tiger-eye. He found Tiger-eye on the road, sneaking up behind a young child. He tried to scoop up the youngster, who didn't run away. But Tiger-eye's hands only reached air.

'What?' puzzled Tiger-eye, and Sword Master watched as the man's hand passed through the child repeatedly. The road lit up with headlights, but Tiger-eye didn't seem to notice. 'It's a hologram! Why is there a hologra...?'

'Look out! Car!' yelled Sword Master, realising with horror that a vehicle was tearing along up the road, straight toward his adopted dad.

The call came too late. Tiger-eye only had enough time to face the oncoming vehicle before it collided brutally with him. The impact flung him onto the sidewalk like a discarded toy. The driver didn't brake and continued to drive on, even laughing out the open window.

Sword Master started to pursue the car, but he realised the better option would be to check on Tiger-eye. He took note of the car's license plate, '6OTCHA', before returning to his dad and his prisoner. She currently lay on the footpath, under the effect of Sword Master's blowgun tranquilliser.

'Crime-fighting's over for the night,' grunted Tiger-eye, sounding strained. 'We need to get back home... now.' He stood up, wiping the blood away from the corners of his mouth. He braced one shoulder as he began walking.

It seemed that, along with his other abilities, Tiger-eye possessed the nine lives of a cat. To Sword Master, that was the only explanation as to how he could've survived such an impact.

Sword Master pulled out a tiny camera from his utility belt and attached it to the shoulder of the lady's black long-sleeve shirt. Then, he checked his phone to make sure the camera was linked to it.

Tiger-eye limped away, and Sword Master followed, dragging his prisoner behind him. Sword Master planned to interrogate her, determined to figure out who was building the weapons and how they would be utilised. They stopped a couple of streets down, where a quietly idling car waited for them.

Sword Master realised it was autonomous when he couldn't find a driver. He never knew his adopted dad designed such advanced cars, but it was obvious he'd summoned the car from Power Mansion. The word 'power' was scrawled across the doors of the car in fancy writing.

Tiger-eye stepped into the backseats of the car, and Sword Master followed, seating his prisoner next to him. Sword Master noticed Tiger-eye sitting statue-still with eyes closed, and he didn't want to interrupt if his dad needed to concentrate on something. He pressed his lips closed and stared at his prisoner instead of talking.

The car accelerated with a sound barely louder than a

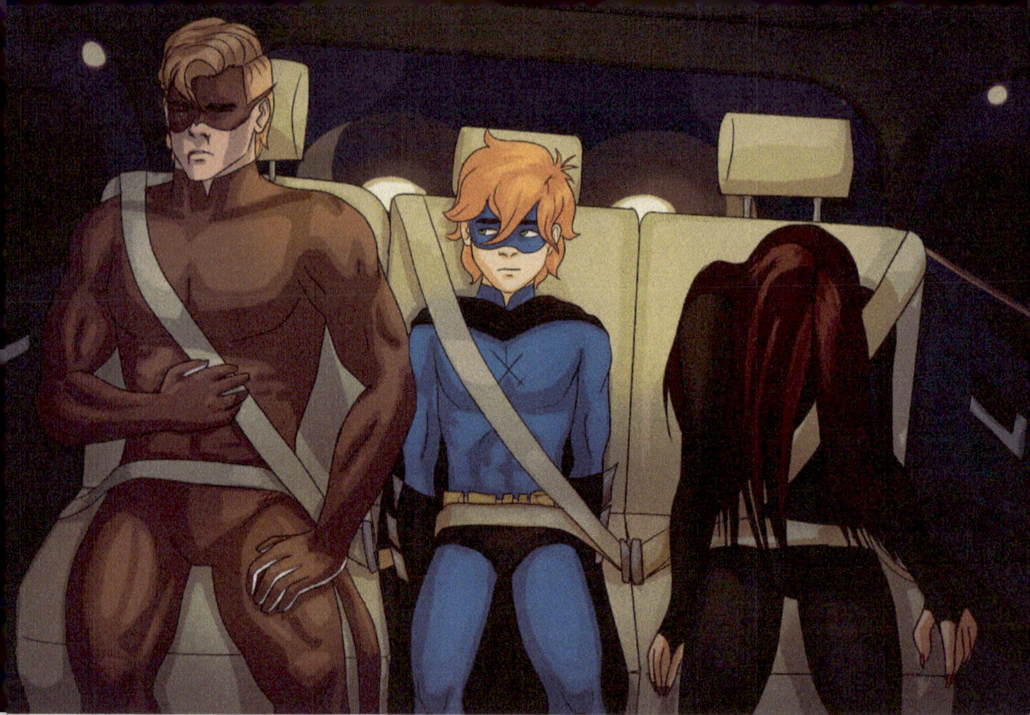

hum, and the windows became so tinted no one would be able to see inside.

Despite the fact the lady had been tranquillised, she wasn't entirely unconscious, and she smiled slightly.

Chapter 14

Injured

Sword Master and Tiger-eye walked quickly up to Power Mansion's front door, each step becoming more difficult for Tiger-eye as his injuries began to affect him. He couldn't concentrate on lessening his pain anymore; it had increased too much for him to control.

'Go up to bed now,' he instructed, summoning Grandfather by pressing a button on the wrist of his costume, which activated a silent alarm. As Sword Master ran upstairs, carrying his prisoner with him, Grandfather entered the room, rubbing the sleep out of his eyes.

'What's wrong?' asked Grandfather.

'I got hit by a car,' replied Tiger-eye, breathing heavily. He wrapped his arms around his middle, sinking to the floor as he coughed up more blood. 'I'll explain later...'

'Let's get you to the medical room, preferably before it's too late and we can't get you to move at all.'

Grandfather helped Tiger-eye to rise to his feet, and they journeyed to the medical room.

'I don't want... the boys to see me like this...' he forced out, as Grandfather set up a stretcher. Tiger-eye collapsed onto it.

'Fine,' agreed Grandfather, just to make his patient happy. 'Can you do the mind thing?' He gestured to his head as though not really understanding how it was done. 'It might help you manage.'

'I already tried. Didn't last long enough,' Tiger-eye settled down but still struggled to breathe normally, describing pain in his chest as the cause. Grandfather began taking X-rays to check if there were any broken bones, and various other scans to diagnose the other injuries.

'Let me know when you need painkillers.'

'You think I'll need them?' questioned Tiger-eye, noticing the use of 'when' rather than 'if'.

'If this is only the beginning of that delayed response to injuries stuff, then yes.'

Attempt for Answers

Up in his room, Sword Master lowered the lady to the ground, removing the gag from her mouth. She slowly opened her eyes, still sleepy from the tranquilliser Sword Master used to capture her.

'You need to give me some answers,' he demanded, his hands bursting into flame. 'Who is your boss?'

'He would kill me if I told you,' pouted the lady. Silently, she pressed a button on a tiny device hidden in her hand. Sword Master caught the movement out of the corner of his eyes and batted it away.

'I will make you wish you'd died if you don't tell me,' he countered, his hand inching closer to her face.

'Okay, okay, I don't even know his name,' admitted the lady reluctantly. 'He's a super-intelligent kid, maybe slightly older than you. And he hides in shadows all the time.'

'What's he planning?'

'I don't know. He doesn't tell anyone his plans, and I'm only his weapon-tester and hologram realism designer,' she answered, moving as far away from the flames as possible.

'Hologram...?' mused Sword Master, remembering Tiger-eye's surprised voice just before the car hit him. 'You set up Tiger-eye for the car to hit!' Anger welled up inside him, and he struggled to control it.

'Guilty as charged,' smirked the lady. 'The job pays well.'

'You think this is funny?' The fire on his hands flared enough that some of the lady's thick, dark hair caught alight. Sword Master concentrated hard as the flames devoured the majority of the length. Then, he snuffed it out by thought alone, leaving the hair blackened and brittle. The lady brought her hand up to it, and just the touch of her fingers destroyed it into a fine dust.

'Congratulations. You've just earned yourself a reason not to mess with me,' he continued calmly. 'Next time, the consequences of angering me will be much worse for you.'

The lady stared in shock, not wanting to move her eyes in case they saw the mess that was once her beautiful hair.

'You'll pay for that,' muttered the lady. Tears welled in her eyes, which she quickly hid when she raised her face to glare at him. 'You'll pay... with your life.'

'How? You're my prisoner.'

'Oh, naive child,' tutted the lady condescendingly. 'Things just aren't that simple in this life.'

'You sound like you know things you're not telling me,' he frowned. 'Anyway, you're staying here until you give me all the answers I need.'

He secured the lady in a locked cupboard and prepared himself for bed. He knew the lady was hiding information, and he intended to find out what she and her boss were planning, one way or another. Exhausted, Rifle changed out of his costume, jumped into bed and fell asleep.

belt
cape
symbol
ZIM   ME
My Car

Escaped

Rifle woke up as the sun peeked over the horizon. He dressed into his Sword Master costume to check on his prisoner, but the cupboard was empty! Only the torn remains of the ropes binding the lady's wrists and ankles remained. He lifted the ropes in astonishment, examining the ends, which looked as though a laser had cut through them.

'How did she escape?' he wondered aloud. 'I removed all her weapons.' Then, he noticed a piece of notepaper on the ground where the ropes had been.

'Dear Captor, I know who you are. Also, I lied about not knowing my boss's identity. I'm his most trusted assistant. You won't catch me again, not while I'm alive. So goodbye, Sword Master/Rifle Power. — N.S.'

Although the note didn't exactly state any threats, Rifle felt a twinge of fear. How did the lady know both his names? What was she hiding about her boss? Would she try to kill him like she'd said while still imprisoned? Rifle shivered, dropping the ropes back into the cupboard, then getting changed into his school uniform. Racing downstairs, he stuffed his breakfast down his throat as quickly as he could. He ran up to Grandfather, who just exited the room where Tiger-eye lay.

'Where's Dad?'

'He doesn't want you to see him,' replied Grandfather, trying to move past. Rifle blocked his path.

'Why not? Is he okay?'

'Please Rifle,' sighed Grandfather, 'Let me pass. Haven't you got school to attend?'

'Yes, but my father comes first.'

Rifle was shocked at how much Tiger-eye's condition had worsened quickly during that night. Grandfather's analysis showed many broken ribs close to puncturing the lungs, fractured collarbone and severe bruising of the torso. Tiger-eye's sprained ankle and jarred wrist were the least of his worries.

Grandfather remained cool, calm and collected while treating Tiger-eye, although seeing the usually strong man like this disturbed Rifle. Grandfather offered Tiger-eye some breakfast.

'I can't eat it,' Tiger-eye turned his head away from the

bowl of cereal. 'Just give me... some time.' Grandfather inserted a drip to ensure the injured man would receive the required nutrients and hydration needed for recovery.

'James, we'll need to remove your costume to apply bandages, but if you move, you could do more damage to yourself,' began Grandfather. 'I'm going to have to cut the suit off you.'

'But that would wreck it,' protested Tiger-eye, slowly reaching up and pulling off his mask.

'I can make a new suit, but I can't make a new you,' resolved Grandfather, proceeding to remove the Tiger-eye costume.

'I'll be fine,' grumbled James. 'I can heal, the suit can't.' Once the task was completed, Grandfather and Rifle could see the dark purple bruising that spread painfully over the man's toned abs and chest. Grandfather started applying soothing cream to help the healing process and numb the ache.

Rifle turned away to try and stop the rising nausea, and after a few deep breaths, he felt better. He made sure to avoid glancing at the bruising for the rest of the time he stood in the room. It helped when Grandfather slid a loose blue T-shirt over James' head and assisted James in pulling it over his chest and arms until the shirt was on properly.

'It's ironic,' James gave a quiet chuckle. 'The person who

drove into me was driving one of the vehicles I designed: the Power Ahead.' James owned a business that built a brand of car, the Power, which he invented. The business, called Power Autos, produced many different models, each with different purposes. The most popular cars included the Luxury, for driving in comfort and style; the Sonic, for fast driving; and the Ahead, which possessed the most powerful engine for hauling heavy loads.

'You have a warped sense of humour,' responded Grandfather, shaking his head dolefully.

'What else would there be to laugh about?' James twisted his pain-filled face into a wan smile. 'I'm trying to distract myself. Having you guys here helps,' he moved his arm just enough to touch Rifle's hand.

Rifle smiled back, but he wasn't fully concentrating. He pulled out his phone to view a live recording of his escaped prisoner's actions. Since he'd planted a tiny camera on the lady, he could watch and hear everything she said and did. He decided he would talk to James later about the note from the frequency ray lady.

Unusual Events

The lady approached her boss, the mysterious teenager.

'I let myself be captured, so Sword Master brought me into his house,' explained the lady. 'I set up a scanning system that will allow you to view the layout of the bedrooms in the mansion, and I got a recording of Sword Master's voice, as you requested.'

'Very good,' nodded the teen, pleased. He knew she wouldn't be able to see if he'd smiled, and it would all contribute to the enigmatic identity he'd built for himself. 'You may leave now.'

The lady placed the recording device on the table in front of the teenager before leaving. He picked up the device, giving a little snicker.

'This will be perfect to alter to my advantage,' he closed his fingers around the device. 'Everything is going exactly to plan.'

He stared expectantly at a monitor showing security camera views around his building. A certain young teen would be arriving for an interview any moment now.

He rolled back his sleeve to reveal a complex watch. Dozens of buttons and switches were packed into the small surface around the clock face. Pressing his thumb and middle finger on the sides, he held his forefinger over the glass face. Blue light scanned over it, authorising his fingerprint.

It didn't appear as though anything had changed, but now he could not be recognised as his former self. The twins had only been young when they'd last seen him, but he never underestimated the power of young minds.

Without his cloaking device, he considered the probability of his identity being discovered too high. The device would trick anyone's mind into being unable to find a resemblance. Even with a photo held up next to his face, the connection between his past self and current self could not be made.

A young teenager with an unmistakable orange mullet appeared in one camera view.

'Come in,' called the villain without turning around. His voice transferred to a speaker near the younger teen, prompting the newcomer to enter.

'Welcome, Flame. Or would you prefer your real name, Tyler?'

'How did you know...?' Flame's jaw dropped.

'Step 1 when working for me: Get used to the fact I know everything about you,' smirked the shadowed villain.

'Um, I'd prefer Flame, not Tyler,' confirmed Flame, still slack-jawed. 'You *are* going by the name of Killer Kaine, aren't you? Just making sure.'

'Yes.'

A thought seemed to occur to Flame.

'If you know everything about me, then why call me for an interview?'

'I prefer to hear you answering my questions aloud. It's different from mindreading because of your tone of voice and involuntary muscle movements that give away so much about you,' explained Killer Kaine. Flame looked more than a little intimidated, no doubt about the fact that Killer Kaine could read his mind. 'First question. What is the reason for you coming to work for me?'

'I want to gain James' attention and prove to him how awesome I am. That I'm capable of anything Rifle can do and more. That my way earns more money. Rifle works stupid long hours, and I don't see the point in that when you can earn quick money like you advertised in that job offer,' answered Flame, talking quickly due to nerves. 'You're, like, the most powerful crime boss of the underworld, so I kinda think you're capable of getting the money.'

'Ah, jealous of your twin and competitive. Interesting. Your logic is twisted, unrefined and inefficient, but I can work with that,' replied Killer Kaine. 'Second question. Would you do anything I tell you to do?'

'Well, as long as it's not...' Flame stopped. 'I would,' he reconsidered, seeming to remember just who he was talking to.

Killer Kaine knew he'd been going to say, 'as long as it's not a wrong command', which was something the twins had been told by their mother for the first six years of their life.

'You don't need to be concerned about those controlling tactics and rules,' Killer Kaine waved a hand carelessly. 'They only hold you back from accomplishing greater things.'

'Mm-hm,' nodded Flame in acceptance, but he still looked doubtful.

Flame would be more difficult than most other villains. His morals were not entirely goody-goody, but he did oppose killing. That was something he needed to get used to, although it could take a long time to break through the characteristic stubbornness.

'If I am to hire you, I need your full obedience...'

'But I thought you said obedience doesn't matter,' frowned Flame, confused.

'Obeying my commands is for your own good,' murmured Killer Kaine, staring deep into Flame's eyes. 'Unlike everyone else, I care about whether you live or not.' That much was true; Killer Kaine needed Flame for his plan.

Flame was someone with permission to enter Power Mansion, which would make things a whole lot easier for Killer Kaine. 'This job is perfect for you. Why the hesitation?' With a slow smirk, he added, 'I'll even finish that invisible cape for you.' Killer Kaine stood up quickly, and Flame jumped in shock.

'So, do you still want the job?' asked Killer Kaine, speaking in normal tones now.

'Absolutely,' Flame blinked, rubbing his head and no doubt wondering why he suddenly felt so certain about taking the job. 'It sounds perfect for me.'

'Then congratulations. The position is yours,' Killer Kaine smiled like a viper as he ushered Flame out of the room. 'Come back in an hour, and I'll have your first task ready for you.'

The cloaking device had worked like a charm, aided by the shadows in the room. Killer Kaine couldn't have been happier with the results. Also, the brainwashing test was a success. With only subtle mind control, Flame was all his.

*　　*　　*

When Rifle returned home from school that afternoon,

he dumped his backpack on the floor and dashed past Grandfather, heading straight for James' room.

'Dad? Are you in here?'

As quickly as possible, James pulled his shirt down over his torso to hide the bruising.

'Rifle, I thought Grandfather would've told you to stay out,' frowned James as he entered.

'I just had to see you. I remembered something really, really important.'

James could sense fear behind his words.

'Okay, what's wrong?' relented James, and rather than sending Rifle away, he patted the bed beside him. Rifle sat tentatively on the side of the bed and began talking.

'I captured that frequency ray lady the other night and tried to get answers from her, but she wouldn't answer. I got angry, which made her angry, and then this morning, I found she'd escaped. She left this note behind,' he explained, handing the paper to James.

'She knows your identity...' murmured James. 'Does she know mine too? Did she tell you what 'N.S.' stands for?'

'No, she didn't provide any names. She said I'd pay for what I did, with my life.'

'This is serious.' James shook his head. 'Your first night,

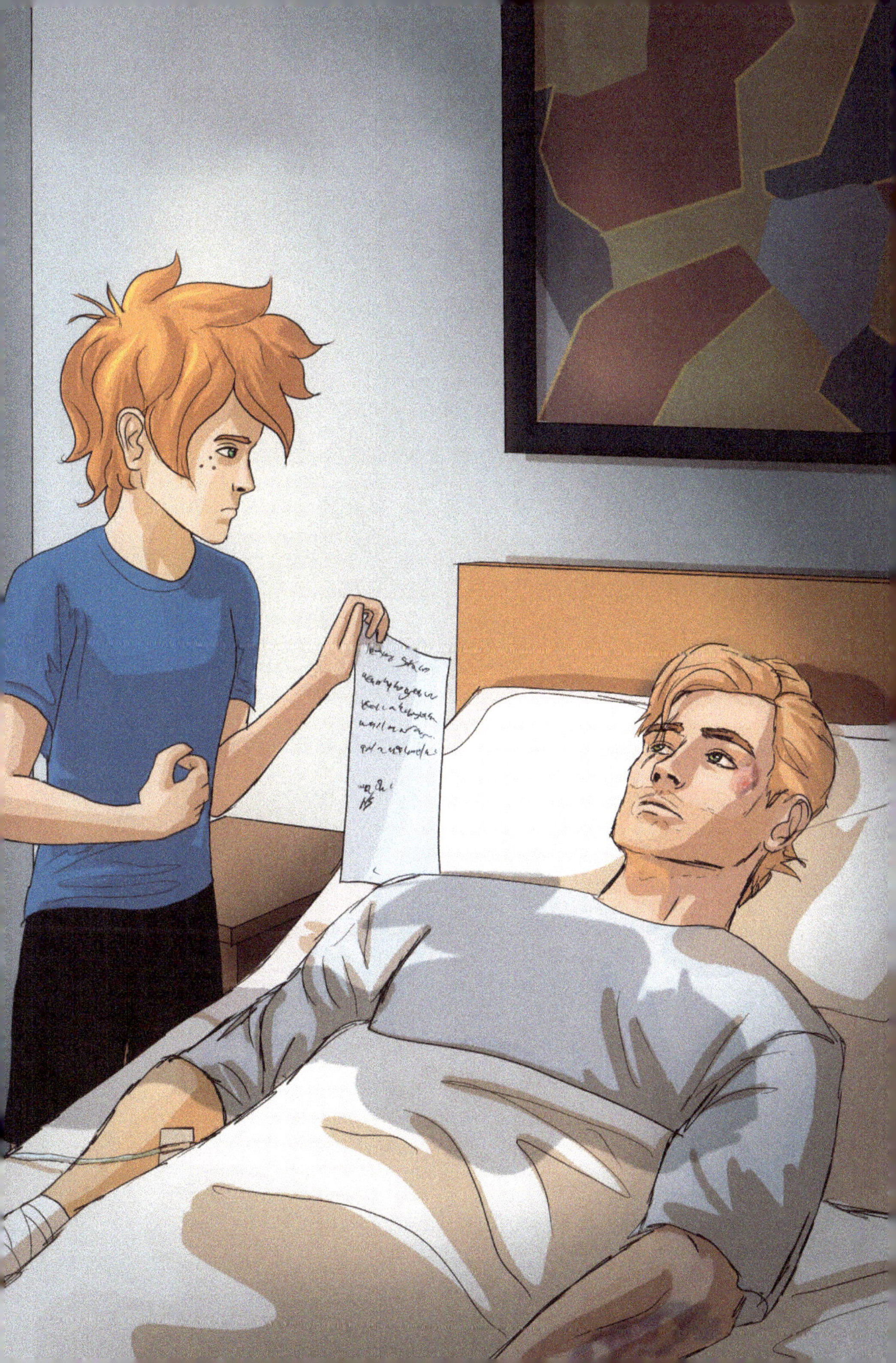

and you've earned an enemy who wants to kill you.' He didn't verbalise the fact that, in his current condition, he wouldn't be able to protect Rifle from the lady or her boss.

'Please don't go out on the streets alone. Make that, don't go out on the streets until I take you. It would be too danger-ous for you otherwise. And Rifle... Eyow!' He finished in a yelp, one of his hands jerking as though something stung it. The hand flopped uselessly to his pillow, and James brought his opposite hand toward it, reaching at the air inaccurately while trying to scratch the 'itch'. That hand, too, went limp.

'Rifle... get... out...' His speech became almost incoherent, his eyelids lowering. He jerked them open again to peer up at Rifle with glazed over eyes. 'Sstronggg... tranquilllizzzerrr... veryyy... faaa...' His voice faded, and his eyes closed.

'Dad?' gaped Rifle, head whipping from side to side as he tried to work out what happened. 'Dad, answer me!' He slapped James' face and shook the unconscious man's shoulders desperately. The only response was a sleepy grunt of pain from the jolting action.

Rifle released James and stepped back, shaking his head in disbelief.

'Grandfather!! Grandfather, come here!' He thought he could hear muffled footsteps exiting the room, but soon,

Grandfather's hurried footsteps drowned out the other sound.

'What's wrong? What are you doing in here?'

'Something's happened to Dad. He's suddenly fallen asleep like he's been tranquillised, but no one was in here except me.' Grandfather inspected James carefully.

'He's unharmed, but it must've been a powerful sedative to have acted so quickly,' concluded Grandfather. 'So, you say no one was in here?'

'No one I could see,' confirmed Rifle, secretly wondering if the footsteps he heard belonged to the culprit. He whipped out his phone again as a notification buzzed to make him aware of new activity in his live recording.

The view on his phone was different to usual, and Rifle realised that the camera had fallen from the lady's shirt onto the ground. It wouldn't affect his spying too much, because luckily, the camera lay in the correct room and faced the lit area. Rifle watched intently as a caped figure entered the villains' meeting area.

Chapter 18

The Scheme

'Flame,' greeted Killer Kaine from the shadows. 'What is your report?' Flame approached the teen almost nervously, tugging the longer hair of his mullet.

'This tranquilliser works fast... even on Tiger-eye. He fell asleep before a minute passed,' replied Flame, handing over the dart gun. 'Also, the invisible cape worked perfectly; Sword Master didn't see me.' Next, the lady with burnt hair entered the room.

'Ninja Star,' Killer Kaine nodded to her. 'I received your written report of the frequency ray.'

'Okay,' acknowledged Ninja Star. She paused before continuing, 'Like I've said before, Sword Master kidnapped me and tried to find out about you, Kaine.'

'It's Killer Kaine,' snapped the teen moodily.

'Sorry,' cringed Ninja Star. 'I didn't give him any answers, even though he threatened me with fire and burned here.'

She pulled aside a thick curtain of hair to reveal a large patch of hair on one side of her head now shaved short. She'd obviously done the best job she could to keep her hair looking beautiful, parting it differently to cover the shaved area. 'He's got a quick temper.'

'I see,' accepted Killer Kaine. With a hint of humour, he added, 'The new style suits you.'

Ninja Star opened her mouth to comment but was interrupted by a muscular man bounding boisterously into the area.

'I hit 'im, I did,' celebrated the man. 'Tiger-eye was there on the road, an' me an' me car hit 'im, bam, straight on!'

'That's nice, but what have I told you about being quiet?' responded Killer Kaine.

'I'm meant to be it so we don't upset the neighbours,' remembered the man.

'Exactly,' nodded Killer Kaine.

'Hey, why'd he not die? I floored the pedal,' The man scratched his head, adding even more tangles to his hair.

'Tiger-eye is a superhero,' Ninja Star huffed as she crossed her arms. 'He's obviously trained himself to survive these things.'

'That, and I installed a limiter on the engine,' clarified

Killer Kaine. 'The limiter set the Ahead's speed to just fast enough to injure someone with above-average strength, without killing him.'

'But why don't you want-?' began the man.

'I thought you wanted him...' said Ninja Star at the same time.

'Uh-uh-uh, no more questions. The less you know about my plans, the better,' interrupted Killer Kaine. 'This is all on a need-to-know basis. You both don't need to know.'

The man and Ninja Star shut their mouths.

'Now, Tekno, I have a job for...'

'Who's Tekno?' interrupted the man, confused.

'That's you, silly,' scowled Killer Kaine.

'But that's not my name, my name is...'

'It's your code name,' sighed Killer Kaine in exasperation. 'Here, you're going to be called Tekno.'

'Oh, right.' Tekno grinned sheepishly, fidgeting with his already messy shoulder-length black hair.

'So, Tekno, this job involves you and Ninja Star working together. We want to make sure Tiger-eye can't continue to train Sword Master. Do not kill either of them. I will be the one to do it when the time is right.'

'Yes sir,' chorused Ninja Star and Tekno, leaving to begin their task.

Killer Kaine paused a moment, and his eyes flicked to the camera on the floor. The side of his mouth twitched, making a dimple appear beside his mouth for a split-second.

Rifle swallowed hard from where he watched in the safety of his room. That villain always gave him the creeps.

Killer Kaine waited until the others were gone before moving over to a set of drawers. He pulled out a picture frame and stared at the picture inside. Rifle strained to see the image from his phone screen, but the camera was at the wrong angle.

'I know you understood my need for freedom, Mum,' he spoke to the picture. 'No one else did. Dad, the boys, all so insistent on forcing me into things I never wanted to do.' Killer Kaine's face twisted in anger. 'So why did *you* have to die when you're the only one I wanted alive!' He stopped himself from slamming the frame to the floor, quickly shoving it into its drawer instead.

Rifle got the sickening feeling that Killer Kaine was about to speak straight to him, as the villain kneeled down in front of the camera.

'You and Tyler might be the only ones alive in the family,

Rifle, but you're going to wish you died in that fire.' He gave a creepy, slow smile before deliberately standing up and leaving the camera alone.

Rifle's heart beat quickly in his chest. Something about that teenager gave him a feeling of impending doom. He felt glad the camera was okay, but knowing that Killer Kaine had spotted it spoilt things somewhat. Killer Kaine would probably stop giving truthful information, therefore rendering the camera useless.

Suddenly, Killer Kaine reappeared close to the camera.

'Stop trying to spy on me,' hissed the villain. 'This is your first and last warning.' Like squashing a bug, Killer Kaine crushed the camera with one thumb, and Rifle's live recording went black. Rifle nearly jumped out of his skin.

Spooked, Rifle sprinted to the medical room, where James was slowly beginning to wake up. Despite the fact Rifle desperately wanted to talk to James, he hesitated outside the doorway. He began having second thoughts about telling James any of the events he'd just witnessed. James wouldn't be able to help anyway, and hearing everything would just worry the man unnecessarily.

'Grandfather, what just happened?' James mumbled groggily, rubbing his face.

'You were hit by a tranquilliser dart on your left hand. The dart seemed to vanish before we could study it.'

'So, you can't work out who did it,' murmured James, closing his eyes. 'It's probably just a prank of Tyler's.'

Grandfather knew James wasn't thinking clearly yet, so he didn't comment.

'Where's Rifle?' asked James.

'I think he's still asleep,' replied Grandfather. James

heaved himself into an upright position, pushing through the pain.

'I can't let him take on the villains,' grunted James, obviously not listening to Grandfather. 'He's too irrational, dangerous even, to be training alone. I need to speak to him. Now.'

'No. I must insist that you rest. You are no good to him like this. I will check on him myself.'

Rifle sneaked back to his bedroom. Tiger-eye couldn't

help. This was up to him. He changed into his Sword Master costume and leaped out his window. When Grandfather arrived at Rifle's bedroom, it was empty. Rifle, as Sword Master, had already fled into the night, out of earshot and out of sight.

Revelation

Sword Master prowled the streets, his sword at the ready. He wouldn't stop crimefighting just because Tiger-eye told him to. He could handle himself out in the big world, he knew. He intended to find that villain, Killer Kaine, and put a stop to the terrifying schemes.

Sword Master returned to the building where he'd last seen Killer Kaine and the other villains, and he found the window again. Standing on his tiptoes, he watched the scene.

'What is your report now?' enquired Killer Kaine, watching Ninja Star enter.

'We haven't needed to intervene yet,' replied Ninja Star. 'The old man has been preventing Tiger-eye from moving, to 'help him heal faster'.'

'He is doing the work for us,' smirked Killer Kaine.

'Unfortunately, it's not stopping Sword Master,'

continued Ninja Star, cringing away from Killer Kaine's glare. 'He's training without Tiger-eye's assistance.'

'It sounds like he needs to come down with a mysterious sickness. It should keep him from doing anything for a couple of weeks,' replied Killer Kaine. 'By then, I will be ready to destroy them both.'

'Um... I'm just wondering, why aren't you ready now?' asked Ninja Star.

'Are you questioning my plans?' Killer Kaine frowned dangerously.

'N-no, of course not,' stammered Ninja Star. She quickly recovered herself. 'I'll make sure to get this 'sickness' to Sword Master.' With a bow of her head, she began to leave.

'I'm counting on your success, Ninja Star. Do not fail me,' warned Killer Kaine, and Ninja Star paused only long enough to nod before closing the door behind her.

Flame slowly approached Killer Kaine.

'I didn't know all this was to kill Tiger-eye and Sword Master,' began Flame sadly. 'I mean, it was fun testing out the weapons and tech on them, but...'

'You disappoint me,' stated Killer Kaine with a shake of his head. 'I thought you could do better than this.'

'I don't want them dead,' insisted Flame. 'If this is what it comes to, then I quit.' Killer Kaine's eyes hardened.

'How dare you, you traitor,' he spat. 'Get out of my sight!' Flame turned and sprinted out of the room. Sword Master quickly hid behind a nearby dumpster, peeking out to witness Flame stopping just outside the building.

'Well, it was good while it lasted,' sighed Flame, taking off his mask to reveal the face of Tyler. 'I just can't allow my brother and my guardian to die.'

Sword Master stifled a gasp. *My brother, Tyler, is Flame? He's working with Killer Kaine?* He stared in shock for a while, watching as Tyler walked off.

Before he could get his wits about him, Sword Master heard Grandfather's voice in his head.

'Rifle, come back,' pleaded the voice. 'James is worried about your safety and could hurt himself further by trying to bring you back.'

Sword Master shook his head to clear the words echoing around.

'I'm fine out here,' he protested out loud, but his conscience got the better of him.

Meeting with Fiona

Sword Master returned to Power Mansion, wondering how Grandfather's voice entered his head like that.

'Okay, I don't know how you did it,' he sighed as he marched past Grandfather, not meeting his eyes. 'But it was creepy, and I also don't know why I came back.'

'You came back because you cared,' Grandfather replied with a warm smile. 'And don't worry, I just used some special technology to send messages to your mind, not anything to be 'creeped out' about.'

Without commenting, Sword Master stomped upstairs to his room. *I'm not meant to care,* he thought angrily. *I'm a walking, talking crimefighting machine. Grandfather just doesn't get it.*

He ripped the costume off his body, changing into his other clothes. *Fine, if I can't go out, I'll just continue training... my way.* Now as Rifle, he grabbed his swords and

moved into the training area. Angrily slashing his favourite weapons through the air, he wondered how he'd got
himself into such a mixed-up situation.

Tyler was a villain. Killer Kaine was planning to give Rifle
some kind of sickness, and in the end, both James and Rifle
would die.

'Why does this happen to me?' Rifle stabbed a punching
bag before sitting on the ground hopelessly. He needed to
tell James about what he'd heard; he just had to find the
right time to do it.

*　*　*

'A lady named Fiona Dan just called, requesting a meeting with you,' Grandfather informed James at breakfast. 'She seems to have an urgent matter she wishes to discuss with you.'

'Did she tell you what was so important?'

'No, she wanted to talk to you in person,' Grandfather rolled his eyes. 'Ms Dan was very specific on that part.'

'When does she want to meet?' asked James tiredly. Not sleeping well since receiving his injuries, the last thing he felt like doing was seeing people. He'd set up a rigorous rehabilitation program for himself and intended to start straight after breakfast. He hoped the meeting wouldn't clash with the program.

'Ms Dan insisted sometime this afternoon, and she suggested 3:00pm,' explained Grandfather.

'This... afternoon...' choked James. He cleared his throat before continuing in a more normal tone, 'Tell her I can't see her.'

'She won't take no for an answer,' added Grandfather.

'Ugh,' scowled James. After a few seconds of thought, he relented. 'I'd better start preparing myself then.' He stood, and with Grandfather's assistance, he readied himself for the pushy businesswoman's meeting, which would be in a few hours. When he'd gathered everything he needed and dressed into casual but neat clothes, James sat on his bed and closed his eyes to block out his constant pain. Vaguely, he heard Rifle entering the room.

'Let me come to the meeting, too,' begged Rifle.

'No.'

'Please? If I am going to be the heir, I need to start learning the business. I'm thirteen now.'

'Where's your brother? Sleeping late again, I assume.'

Rifle was silent and James mistook it for sulking.

'Fine,' he conceded, just wanting Rifle to stop bothering him. 'But not one word while I'm trying to concentrate, understood?' Rifle gave a grin and left James alone.

When the time came, Rifle helped James settle at the office table, sending Grandfather to bring Fiona inside. The lady strutted in with ridiculously high-heeled shoes, leading a sensibly dressed young teenage girl behind her.

'Hi, I'm Fiona,' introduced the lady, extending a hand to James. With a billion-dollar smile that made most ladies weak at the knees, James shook her hand, covering the fact that the movement hurt. Fiona's eyes widened when she saw Rifle, but she did not offer her hand.

'I'm James. Nice to meet you,' replied James politely.

'This is my niece, Tilly,' Fiona smiled down at the girl, who only looked bored in return. 'She's here to see how things work in businesses like ours.' Tilly met Rifle's eyes, and suddenly, her attitude changed to keen interest.

'It seems we both have the same idea,' nodded James. 'Let's discuss the business. What did you want from me?'

As Fiona began talking, Tilly leant towards Rifle.

'Hi,' grinned Tilly. 'Do you find this stuff as boring as I do?'

'It depends how much you find it boring,' answered Rifle. 'I actually asked to be here.'

'You're Mr Power's son, right?'

'Yes, although I'm technically one of two sons. I'm Rifle.'

'Nice to meet you, Rifle,' responded Tilly. 'Oh, I forgot, Aunty Fiona brought cookies.'

'I don't eat cooki...'

'They're low fat, low sugar and amazingly delicious,' interrupted Tilly keenly. 'Aunty Fiona created the recipe herself, and I baked them this morning.'

'Look, I'm not going to eat any, but Dad might,' Rifle finally got a word in. 'He sometimes eats my homemade goodies and gives feedback. If you wanted feedback on the recipe, you could give a cookie to him.'

'Okay,' agreed Tilly. 'I guess there's always room for

improvement.' She and Rifle sat up straight as Fiona pushed back her chair to leave.

'Where's she going?'

'She forgot papers that she left in the car,' explained James. Rifle noticed a hint of irritation on his dad's face and wished he'd listened to Fiona's reason for coming. It was probably something pathetic; that would annoy James.

'What did she want to come here for?'

'She wanted to buy bulk of the Power Sonic for her business,' frowned James. 'Hardly an urgent matter like she made it out to be.'

'Would you like to try one of the cookies I made?' asked Tilly, holding out the platter.

'What's in them?' questioned James with a smile. 'I'm sure Rifle would've told you I give advice for improving the recipes.' Tilly began listing the ingredients.

'You know, I wouldn't have thought those ingredients would go so well together,' commented James, swallowing the last of the cookie. 'That's either a great recipe, or you're an incredible chef.'

'A bit of both,' grinned Tilly cheekily. 'I'm glad you liked it.' She seemed to notice the various scrapes and bruises on James' skin for the first time, and she gave him a quizzical look. 'How'd you get those impressive bruises?'

'Oh, I tripped on the staircase and landed on the railing,' explained James, demonstrating the action while he spoke. 'Broke a couple of ribs while I was at it, too.' He gave a sheepish grin. 'What can I say? I wasn't looking where I was going.'

Tilly giggled, and Rifle marvelled at how easily James had lied about his injuries. Tilly obviously believed him.

James straightened up as Fiona entered. 'Did you find the paperwork?'

'Yes, thanks. They must've slipped under the passenger seat,' Fiona held up a stack of papers before placing them

in front of James.

Tilly reached for one of her cookies herself, but Fiona slapped her hand away.

'Don't touch! They're for our hosts. Where are your manners?'

'But I made the cookies,' protested Tilly, eyes wide.

'She can eat some,' offered James, holding out the plate toward Tilly. 'We certainly won't be eating all of these.'

'Tilly, you're not having any,' insisted Fiona, with such a finality that Tilly stopped reaching for the plate.

Once Fiona seemed satisfied that Tilly wouldn't eat one, she turned back to James and continued to discuss the business paperwork with him. He politely signed the necessary papers, although it was obvious to Rifle he didn't want to encourage Fiona's pushy behaviour.

When they finished a few minutes later, Fiona and Tilly prepared to leave.

'Rifle, have you tried one of Tilly's cookies?' asked Fiona as they made their way to the front door. 'They're truly delicious.'

'No, I don't want one thanks,' declined Rifle. 'They look yummy, but I'm not eating any.'

'Suit yourself,' shrugged Fiona, stepping into her car

with a flick of her hair. Rifle couldn't stop staring at Fiona when he noticed one side of her hair was short underneath the section she'd lifted... The same side he'd burned on the frequency ray lady. Could Fiona be that lady?

'What?' demanded Fiona, obviously feeling Rifle's eyes watching her.

'Oh... nothing,' Rifle looked away.

Fiona drove off with Tilly, and Rifle noted the number-plate: '6OTY0U'.

Deadly Sickness

Chills ran down Rifle's spine.

He ran inside the house to James.

'Dad, I think Fiona's the lady I kidnapped,' panted Rifle. 'I saw the hair... It was the same!'

'I-I'm sorry,' apologised James, 'I don't feel too good...' Rifle glanced up at his face, startled by how deathly pale James looked. His eyes were unfocused, and he seemed to be struggling to keep his balance. 'Excuse me.' James staggered to the nearest bathroom and was violently sick.

'Grandfather!' yelled Rifle. 'Dad's sick!' His pulse raced. Could this be the sickness that Killer Kaine talked about? How did James get it instead of him?

Grandfather came running and Rifle led him to James.

'What have you done to yourself now?' he muttered, not out of irritation, but out of concern.

'I don't know what happened,' panicked Rifle. 'One

moment, he was fine, the next... like this.'

When James calmed down, Rifle helped Grandfather take him to the medical room.

'I'm okay,' James tried to insist, shrugging off their hands, but he could hardly stand upright and practically fell back into their arms.

That night, James' temperature soared, and he couldn't keep any food down. Soaked in perspiration, he was shivering and delirious.

'He's gonna die,' whispered Rifle, distraught. 'I don't want him to die.' He knew this was one of the stages of Killer Kaine's plan, and if the sickness didn't kill James, then the villains would.

'He won't die,' opposed Grandfather, just to keep Rifle quiet. But he felt secretly worried about how high James' temperature was rising. It was reaching dangerous levels. Rifle dabbed a wet cloth over James' forehead, attempting to cool the desperately ill man.

'Please don't die,' he whispered, grasping James' hand tightly. He couldn't help shivering in the air-conditioned climate, which was deliberately cold to try and lower James' temperature.

'Don't hurt Rifle!' James cried out, as he stared, unseeing, at the ceiling. 'Leave him alone!'

'I'm here, Dad, I'm okay,' reassured Rifle, quickly moving closer to James and hugging his arm to his chest. He stayed like that until James drifted into a fitful sleep, and Grandfather told him to go to his own bed.

'You have school tomorrow,' reminded Grandfather.

'But Dad needs me,' protested Rifle, reluctantly releasing James and standing up.

'You need sleep.' Grandfather tousled Rifle's hair lovingly.

'I'll look after James.'

Rifle looked back sadly, then he walked to his bed.

* * *

Tilly watched as Fiona counted the cookies that remained on the platter. One was missing.

'Did anyone eat a cookie?'

'Yes, Mr Power ate one,' nodded Tilly.

Fiona waited until Tilly left before dumping the cookies in the bin. She didn't realise that Tilly stood just outside the door, still watching, listening.

'It was meant for Rifle,' grumbled Fiona. 'The sickness better not kill James, or I'll be in big trouble. The amount that would only make Rifle sick could easily kill James in his current condition.' She gave a frustrated sigh. 'And Rifle didn't even eat one. Boy, what am I going to tell Killer Kaine?'

'Just that,' answered Killer Kaine, seeming to just appear behind her. Fiona's reflexes kicked in and one hand lashed out at him. Killer Kaine caught her wrist, and Fiona withdrew her hand in embarrassment.

'Sorry, you shocked me,' gasped Fiona.

'Nice to see you haven't lost your reflexes,' was the only response.

'Are you going to fire me? I've failed you,' Fiona lowered her gaze.

'You're too good at your job for me to get rid of you,' replied Killer Kaine. 'Besides, you're still doing your part to stop Tiger-eye from training Sword Master. Now, you need to stop Sword Master from training by himself.'

'Thank you so much! You're the best,' gushed Fiona, relieved Killer Kaine wasn't mad at her.

'I know,' smirked Killer Kaine, climbing out the window. 'It's what I strive to be.'

Tilly backed away. Her aunt was deliberately poisoning people through her favourite cookie recipe. Tilly couldn't believe her Aunty Fiona would do such a thing. Retreating to her room, she sat on her bed and hugged her knees to her chest. She felt so guilty about trying to give the cookies to the friendly boy and kind man at Power Mansion. She wouldn't forgive herself if the man died, and it was her fault.

Recovering

Over the next week, James' condition didn't improve, but it didn't worsen either. Rifle hated leaving James to attend school, but Grandfather made him go every day.

All they could do for James was to make sure he stayed hydrated, even though he remained unable to eat anything. Rifle spent all his spare time with him.

'Rifle, Tyler...' James rolled over onto his side to face Rifle.

'Yes Dad, it's okay,' mumbled Rifle, beginning to wake up where he'd dozed off that night beside James.

'What time is it? Where's your brother?' asked James weakly.

'It's been ten days since you became sick, and it's...' Rifle glanced at the glowing figures on his watch, '... about 1:30am. If Tyler's sensible, he's probably in bed and asleep at the moment.' He immediately thought to himself how Tyler was anything but sensible recently. For all he knew, his twin brother could be out causing chaos somewhere as Flame.

'My head's aching like crazy,' groaned James. Something about his tone triggered an exciting thought in Rifle's head.

'Hang on,' Rifle woke up enough to realise what was happening. 'You're actually talking, right? Not just delirious.'

'I... think so.' James rubbed his face. 'You're really there, aren't you? Some of the things I've seen were so life-like... I thought they were real, but it was all so confusing.'

'Yes, I am really here,' confirmed Rifle, reaching out and touching James' forehead with the back of his hand. James' muscles jerked in surprise, and he grabbed Rifle's arm with a surprisingly strong grip considering how sick he'd been.

'Sorry, I didn't mean to startle you. Don't throw me over your shoulder or whatever,' apologised Rifle. 'I was just checking your temperature, and you're feeling a whole lot cooler already.'

'Yeah, I'm a cool dude,' joked James, almost listlessly, as he released Rifle's arm from the vice-like grip. He was only a shell of his former self, his face gaunt and his body nearly depleted of its energy, but he was alive.

'Dad, I've got something I really need to tell you.'

'Can it wait? I feel half-dead at the moment.' James ran

his hands over his eyes, enjoying the cool temperature of his fingers on his feverish skin.

'I don't think it can wait. I waited last week, and it meant you nearly died.'

'Okay, what is it?' James faced Rifle, forcing himself to pay attention.

'A teenager, who calls himself Killer Kaine, is plotting to kill us, and he's weakening us first. The sickness was intended for me, but maybe the villains changed their mind as to who to give the poison to.'

'Villains?'

'Yeah. Killer Kaine, Ninja Star, Tekno and Flame,' listed Rifle, shuddering at the name Flame. He decided he wouldn't tell James about Tyler just yet. 'I don't know why we're being targeted, but we need to find a way to stop ourselves from being killed.'

'Tell me where they are; I'm going there,' James shot up from lying down, shifting his legs to climb out of bed and begin crimefighting right at that moment. 'I can't let them do anything to you.' He grimaced, holding his head and falling back on the mattress with a groan of frustration. 'Ugh. Just give me an eternity and maybe I'll be ready.' He began to slowly ease himself off the mattress, not giving

up despite having nearly died days before.

'I'll get Grandfather.' Rifle stood up and left the room to fetch Grandfather. He knew James was in no condition to be helping him stop the villains.

Grandfather arrived at James' bedside and checked on the sick man. When he tried to ask James questions, the only responses were the bare minimal answers. James didn't seem to want to talk, almost as if that would reserve his energy for crimefighting. Rifle left Grandfather to try reasoning with James, and he returned to his own bedroom.

Rifle knew he needed to stop Killer Kaine and his accomplices before something more serious happened. His physical ability and mental capacity had grown immensely since the beginning of his training with James, but Rifle understood the villains he was dealing with were dangerous. Who knew what they planned and what challenges were to come?

He was barely even a teenager, but the responsibility had fallen on him to protect his new family. He would train for the fight. He would do whatever it took, even if that meant confronting his twin brother and taking the villains down.

Captives of the Killer

Rifle and his adopted dad, James, are kidnapped, but no one knows they're alive! They must find a way to escape, but that proves difficult with high-security rooms, highly trained guards and dangerous weapons at the villain's disposal. Ambitious teenager, Tilly, teams up with Grandfather to capture 'werewolves' that supposedly committed bank robberies. Tilly thinks there's a connection between Rifle and James' disappearances and the werewolves, but how will she be able to prove her theory? And can Rifle find a way to get himself and James free from their captor?

AB SUPERHEROES

Acknowledgements:

I'd like to thank everyone who has helped me get to where I am now.

- Michelle Worthington — for starting me off on the incredible journey to getting my book published
- Sally Odgers — for great tips on how to improve my story
- Brylee Langley — for inspiration, encouragement and helpful advice
- Todd White — for teaching me everything I know about digital art
- Norman Ospina — for helping me with my website and business tips
- Luke Harris – for doing an amazing job of the cover and interior design
- Mum and Dad — for all their support in every area
- Tiana and Joel — for contributing to my ideas and being the best siblings I could hope for
- God — for always being there for me, giving me my abilities and providing me with everything I need

Thank you everyone for all your help; I couldn't have done this without any of you!

Alisa's hobbies include writing and illustrating super-hero stories, playing film score music on the piano, running her YouTube channel, making comics and graphic novels, composing dramatic music, reading, photography and videography.

Alisa's favourite part about writing books is designing the characters. Since she began reading superhero books in 2016, she's been fascinated by a world of superpowers and villains. She used to write stories and make comics about already existing characters, but her family suggested that she develop new characters. From there, Alisa began writing stories with all her own superheroes, villains, places and brand names.